COMING AROUND AGAIN

By Stephanie Watt

First Published in 2022 by Blossom Spring
Publishing
Coming Around Again Copyright © 2022
Stephanie Watt
ISBN 978-1-7398866-3-9
E: admin@blossomspringpublishing.com
W: www.blossomspringpublishing.com
Published in the United Kingdom. All rights
reserved under International Copyright Law.

ABOUT THE AUTHOR

Stephanie Watt lives in a picturesque part of Essex and started writing after her two daughters had grown up and had children of their own. After a career in aviation, working as cabin crew, where she enjoyed seeing many different places and meeting people from all walks of life, Stephanie decided to embark on a new career as an author.

For Stephanie, writing is just like reading a new book - the ideas come into formation as the story grows from her own imagination, and this is a large part of the pleasure she gains from writing. However, her first and foremost desire for her writing is to give enjoyment to those who read her stories. Stephanie feels that this is the pinnacle of what any author can ask for.

To my daughters, Jennifer and Nicola in memory of their wonderful father, Martin.

CHAPTER 1

June Johnson came in, closed the door and heard silence. She wondered; can you actually hear silence? She did, she heard it a lot at this moment. She took off her black hat; she was reluctant to wear one but she remembered how Tom always liked her in a hat, so she decided to go for it and make his send-off complete, his girl in a hat.

She missed Tom, today had been his funeral, a day of highs and lows, when their children remembered the funny things about him and then, in the next minute, they were crying about their Dad. June did not know what she was going to do without him, they had been so close, so in love, so special. He was an extension of herself and the one that was meant for her.

June sat down in her widow's black and stared out of the window.

"Oh Tom, I can't do this. Talk to me, tell me you're there." Still June heard only silence; she had never felt so alone in her life. She thought of the little, silly things that Tom used to do. Some were annoying, admittedly, but her Tom had been a chuckler, a charmer and a friend, as well as the love of her life.

She thought back to their courting days and smiled at remembering him coming to her house. She would run to the door and open it: her stomach would always flip at the sheer good looks of the man she had fallen in love with. They were so young when they met: Tom was an apprentice carpenter and June worked at the local funeral business, where she would comfort people as they came in to arrange funerals for their loved ones. June had no concept that one day, she or Tom would be the one arranging the funeral of the other. June always thought that they would never get old, her and Tom. Occasionally, she would have a younger person's funeral to deal with and that would upset her, making her realise that life was not always fair. Thinking back to the present, she and Tom had had fifty years together so she was certainly not going to say her life had not been fair, they had three lovely children and two wonderful grandchildren.

June looked at the clock, it was nearly six o'clock. She had eaten after the funeral when they all went back to her daughter's house. Her daughter Meghan laid on a good spread: she was the natural hostess of the family. Jane and Paul, the other two, were not great at entertaining. Paul used to be when he was married, but since his divorce and subsequent move to a tiny one-bedroom flat, he had lost the energy and zest that he once had when his life was, what he called, complete. He had come to live with June and Tom just after his separation, they were only too glad to be there for him but both felt sad that any of their children were hurting. Sometimes, June felt almost guilty at her own happiness, which had stretched its way through their life together and never left them. That all-consuming love and tolerance of another person, the fact that anything that person did was good and acceptable, because they loved you, they got you, cared for you and showed their love with every look, action and that is what June and Tom had and they wished it could happen for everyone.

The phone rang. June wanted to ignore it but realised it may be one of the children and she must keep in sight that these people had lost a beloved Dad, she wiped her face and answered the phone.

It was Meghan. "Hello Mum. You OK?"

Meghan heard in her mother's voice that she had been crying. "Hello darling, yes, I'm fine."

"David and I are checking whether you'd like to come here for the weekend?"

June was touched by the kindness of her children, by their concern for her loneliness. "Thanks sweetheart, I may stay here this weekend and do some work in the garden. I have to get used to being on my own now and I feel closer to your Dad while I'm here, so if it's alright to say no?" June worried that her daughter would feel offended, but Meghan was fine with doing whatever her mother wanted to do.

"No, that's fine Mum. But promise me you'll phone if you change your mind, or just need some company?"

"Of course I will darling," June replied. It was a nice feeling to know Meg was on the other end of a phone anytime she felt she needed.

The call ended - Meghan had a million things to do. June remembered that Mum thing, when the children were at home and there were always things that needed attending to. June was sad for her daughter, but also grateful that she had her lovely family around her at this time.

June decided she needed a cup of tea, her stock answer to some of the most stressful times in her life. As she put the kettle on, she looked out at the garden Tom had so lovingly worked on. The roses he had put in for June were a beautiful shade of peach, her favourite colour for a rose. She wanted to think of him, she wanted to feel him with her, because she felt so alone in a world full of people. The kettle clicked off but June decided to walk around the garden and feel close to Tom, by just looking at his work, by looking at what he had done out of love for his wife. The sadness of being alone was worse than the sadness of feeling old and invisible, something June felt every day in society. She remembered the joy of being young, when people would say how pretty she was and men would open doors for her. Although being young and pretty did bring June joy, it was only ever Tom that she really wanted to be pretty for. There had been occasions when she could have betrayed him, there were plenty of men who used to admire her for her long dark hair and slim figure, but as soon as June had met Tom there was only ever one man for her.

June heard the doorbell. She wondered if she could be bothered to answer it. She walked slowly from the garden and on answering the door, was pleased to see her neighbour, Fran.

No words were spoken as Fran put her arms out; June gratefully fell into the cuddle of a friend and neighbour whom she had known for years. Fran knew how hard today had been for June, that the finality of the funeral had left June feeling pure grief.

June started to cry, "Oh Fran, I miss him, I really miss him."

"I know, June," which was all that was necessary to be said.

Fran went through to the kitchen, where she made them both a cup of tea.

"That was a beautiful funeral, June," said Fran as they drank their tea.

"I know, the children did a really good job of arranging it."

The children had wanted to arrange it for their Dad. June was fine with that because it would help ease the pain for them if she let them be personally involved in arranging it. Both women continued to drink their tea silently, Fran aware that just the company was enough for the moment.

"Do you want me to stay?" Fran asked.

"No, thank you Fran, I'll be fine. I have to get used to being on my own at some point. It's strange, but with all the funeral planning and other things to sort out, I haven't really felt so on my own but now there's nothing much left to do, this is when it's going to feel like I'm alone."

"I know, June, but you know I'm always there if you need company. Just knock, OK?"

"Thanks Fran, I really appreciate that."

She gave Fran another hug and walked with her to the door. She was happy in a way to be back on her own, as she could just lose herself in memories of Tom. She went back into the garden and thought about their first garden together: the tiny little cottage they bought a year after they married; after living with June's parents for a year while they saved a deposit, it was like a castle to them. They moved in during the winter, so had to become good at putting a coal fire on, something up until then only their parents knew how to do. The cottage was in need of some renovation, but Tom loved it, he loved putting their little home together and making it ready for their first baby. Meghan arrived in the summer, a big, bouncy, healthy and happy baby, the image of Tom, even down to their unusually long little toes – something he was very proud of.

June sat at the table lost in her memories when the doorbell rang, she wondered if it was Fran coming back for whatever reason. She opened the door to see Mr James, the funeral director the family had dealt with when arranging Tom's funeral. She was slightly surprised to see him but assumed this was a follow up wellbeing visit.

"Oh, hello Mr James, how are you?" She didn't know quite what to say over and above that.

"Hello Mrs Reader, I hope you don't mind me calling unannounced, but I was wondering if I could speak to you about something?" June was even more confused - she was sure she had settled the account, she wondered if something had happened at the funeral that she was unaware of.

"Yes, of course Mr James, please come in. Can I offer you a cup of tea?"

"That would be nice, thank you." Mr James accepted the offer more for June than himself as he knew from experience with the conversation he was about to have, that the recipient of the news he was about to deliver often needed a hot cup of tea for comfort more than he actually wanted one, so he always tended to accept. June made the tea and poured two, she sat at the table opposite Mr James. He began "Mrs Reader..."

June interrupted him "Please, call me June."

He continued "June, I have something to discuss with you that is very unusual and there is no believable way to say it, so I'm just going to dive straight in. I have been a funeral director for many years, as you know from when we spoke during arrangements for your husband's funeral. Over the years I have organised funerals for many bereaved spouses and, every once in a while, and rarely, very rarely I must add, I come across genuine life soulmates. Oh, I know this is a term bandied about, people think they have their soulmate and that is often enough; but there are situations, like yours, where a greater power confirms that you are indeed true soulmates."

June stared at Mr James, thinking although that had been a nice thing to say, it all sounded a bit weird to her, she decided to let him continue with whatever point he was trying to make. "I have been tasked with delivering something special to the bereaved half of the true soulmates I come across."

June suddenly caught on to the fact that a sales pitch was coming up, she didn't have a clue what bereaved "true soulmates" could be tempted to buy, but she had a feeling she was just about to find out.

"June, what I am about to say will make no sense to you whatsoever but I want you to let me finish and then you can ask any questions you want." June was intrigued but suspicious.

"As I said, you have been chosen as a true soulmate of your late husband and as such, it is my task to deliver the news that you have been granted an opportunity to spend some more time with him..."

June interrupted because she now thought that this man was barking mad.

"Mr James," she began, he put his hand up in a gentle manner and continued.

"Please, just let me explain, I know it's going to be strange and there's a lot to take in but let me continue." June just stared at him. He took this as an acknowledgement to carry on. "So, this is how it is. You and your husband, you had a favourite song, a song that was yours, that meant something to you both when you were young, yes?"

"Er... yes..." Mr James raised his hand again.

"Right, well, this is what you get - and whether you choose to use this opportunity is completely up to you, but those chosen for this always do, because it's something that gives them such joy. You, June, have the opportunity to spend time with your late husband, but both of your physical forms will revert to being young. You will be the age you were when you met and all the fun that came with that. To make this happen it really is very simple, you only have to choose a time, play that favourite song you both had, close your eyes and say his name, wait for your husband's voice to say your name then open your eyes. What you see will shock you, so be as prepared as you can but remember that you will have twelve hours a day - hours of your choice - for two weeks with all the same feelings you had when you were both young and as I said, you both will be young. It is a rather magical experience and one that not many people get to have."

June had heard enough of this bunkum. "Mr James, I really don't know what you're talking about, but this all sounds a bit weird to me, I'm really sorry but I'm very tired after today so

I've listened to what you have to say but really would like to get some rest now."

Mr James stood up. "Of course, but before I go, there are just one or two rules pertaining to this. You must never tell anybody about it and your husband must never be seen by your children. Should either of these happen, he will immediately cease to be with you. This is something offered to be shared by you and him alone, not your family. Oh, and obviously, your physical form will always return to what it is now until the same time you see him, each visit will last twelve hours for the duration of two weeks, from the day you get the first visit. Should you hear the song at any other time it will be meaningless, your husband will only come to you when it is you that physically puts the song on, Now, I don't expect any of this to be totally clear as you are still struggling to believe it but please, feel free to phone me, here is a card with my private number on it".

He handed June a business card.

"Give it some thought, June. Like I said, it really is an opportunity only given to a tiny number of people. It all sounds like hocus-pocus, I know, but what have you got to lose giving it a go and what possible reason could there be for me to come here and make this up?"

June thought, *Because you are barking mad?* Mr James put on his coat and walked to the front door. June couldn't wait to get rid of him, but something about the way he looked back and said, "Give it a go, June, it's a beautiful thing," made her double take her own thoughts. She needed to be alone; she needed to think about what had just been said to her and what reason he would have to make something like this up, it would be an act of extreme nastiness for an esteemed funeral director to risk his business by making this nonsense up, but it had to be nonsense, there was no other explanation.

As she shut the door, the first thing she wanted to do was tell Fran all about this strange visit and what had been said, but Mr James had made it clear that telling anybody would negate and cancel any opportunity to see Tom again and, much as it was all a load of tosh, she needed to think it through a lot more before she decided on her next course of action. For now, all she wanted to do was sleep, so she went to bed and had vivid and real dreams about her and Tom when they were young. When she awoke in the morning, she thought again about Mr James's visit and his intensity and decided that it was all hogwash, until she put the radio on and heard the song. It was their song, the one she had thought of when Mr James mentioned playing it, this was too weird. The dreams, now the song, what had she got to lose? She decided to give the nonsense a go that night, but the problem being that she was technically inept and only had an old record player, suddenly she remembered Tom had kept a lot of their old vinyl records in the attic, she hoped the song was there. June decided to have breakfast, then go into the attic and start looking through their records.

In the attic, June sat surrounded by life, by their life, hers and Tom's. She wondered if she was ready to start looking through so many memories. Tom had kept the attic so neat, stacking everything in marked boxes. She immediately saw the box marked "records" but was distracted by the one marked "photos" and could not resist taking her mind to such better times. She grabbed a few photo albums from the box and sat on the floor of the attic. Each album showed the years of the photographs it contained and like yet another omen to the nonsense Mr James had come out with, the album on top was dated the year she and Tom had met. She opened the first page with a feeling of excitement at being reminded of how they looked so long ago: the first photo was taken outside her old house. Tom was carrying her and they were both laughing, that's all she can ever remember doing with Tom, her whole life with him, laughing. The struggles they had were the same as many other couples, but they were always a team, they stood together every single minute and they worked to resolve problems as a couple, but mainly it was laughter that she remembered. The next few photos were also at her parent's house, in the garden playing silly games or posing. June marvelled at her figure, at her beautiful long hair left loose and flowing and at Tom's handsome face and his slim, athletic body. She remembers touching every part of that body and him doing so to hers. They were totally enamoured with each other from the moment they met and that feeling never went away, not at any time in their lives together. Mr James was right about one thing: they certainly were soulmates in June's opinion. Further on in the album there were pictures of them on the beach, two beautiful young people who had had the greatest luck and fortune in the world to have met and made each other's lives complete. June looked at all the albums, the ones that were the years of the children's lives were especially wonderful, to see each of their beautiful children so new and tiny, each child enhancing and making their lives even more complete. She found herself crying and laughing at regular intervals looking at the photographs, everything now was a bit of a roller-coaster for June's emotions after so many years of having Tom and being a couple, where emotions remained fairly constant. Dealing with the vast amount of negativity that his death had brought was proving difficult for June, she wanted him here again so much.

After what must have been a good hour, June suddenly remembered why she had come up to the attic and after some considerable effort to get up off the floor and silently cursing her old bones, she went to the box marked "records" and got ready to delve deep to find their song, when lo and behold, like yet another omen, on top was their song. She picked it up and her fingers traced the title, while her mind became filled with the tune and she could feel Tom's body against hers as they danced to this beautiful and soulful song. They both knew a lifetime would never be long enough for them to spend together and it hadn't been. She felt his hand on her face, his lips on her cheek as they danced. They were lost in their own world whenever they danced to this song, she felt his breath against her face and knew that they would kiss during this dance because they were one, meeting Tom and holding him always made her feel like a complete person. She had had a relationship before him, but it was nothing like what she had found with Tom, her previous boyfriend had been nice but hardly ever made her laugh. When he left her for a workmate, June's pride was hurt but not her heart. June thought about their wedding. It was a perfect day when she finally married the man she loved from the moment they said hello. She thought of the wedding night and the way her family never knew for a moment that her and Tom were no strangers to sex with each other and their wedding night was made special by the fact that they would wake up together and never be apart again. Remembering sex was strange, they stopped making love after Tom became ill, but they cuddled and still kissed and held each other close and would still dance to songs they loved. When they were younger, though their sex life was amazing, they settled into married life and even after the children, June never stopped feeling desire for him. She knew this was so different for many of her friends who seemed to grow tired of their husbands; June never knew what that felt like.

June's thoughts were suddenly interrupted by someone calling out.

"Mum!" She recognised the voice of her eldest child Meghan who had let herself into the house.

June got up and went to the attic hatch. "I'm up here, Meg. I was just looking through old photos at Dad and me."

"Mum, what on earth are you doing getting up there on your own, we can get the things down for you."

"Oh Meghan, it's not a problem. The loft ladder is easy to pull down and I'm only ruddy seventy-four." June hoped this wasn't the way it was going to be. Her children could be bossy but when Tom was around, they didn't usually direct it toward her. Now he was gone, she hoped she wouldn't become a project. She was about to descend the ladder when she remembered what she had gone up there for, she grabbed the record and handed it down to Meghan to hold while she went down the ladder and pushed it away with the rod.

"What's this, Mum - getting sentimental?" Meghan said, as she looked at the record cover. "Yes, it was our favourite record." She didn't even feel tempted to tell her why she had brought it down, as she knew Meghan would be straight down to see Mr James and demand to know why he was harassing her mother. June didn't feel ready to dismiss what Mr James had said just yet, as her trip down memory lane in the attic had made her want to see Tom again, even more than yesterday when his funeral was held.

"Anyway Mum, I just popped round to see whether you wanted to have tea at ours tonight, you can stay over if you want."

"That's really kind, Meg but I do need to sort a few things out."

"Like what?"

"Well, there's Dad's clothes."

"Yes, Dad's clothes, which we could do now if you want, then I can pick you up later. Stay for a few days if you want, Mum."

"That's really sweet, Meg but I really wouldn't mind a little bit of time on my own to... you know..." she tapped her head, "...get lost in a few memories of Dad."

"OK Mum, but don't leave it too long. We all want to see you and we worry. I might have a get together in a couple of weeks. I'll see if Paul and Jane are free, although knowing Paul, he'll have a hot date. He's gone woman mad since he got divorced: I don't think he's been out more than once with the same woman."

Meghan despaired of her brother: he was going

through his second youth, including what he wore. Still, she adored him, she felt protective toward him and it broke her heart for him when he was asked for a divorce by his ex-wife who had met somebody else. She liked seeing Paul, but he wasn't the same as he had been while he was married and she didn't see him much these days. Neither did June. Occasionally he would call in on his way to or from somewhere; he didn't stay too long but while he was there, he certainly lit June's world up. He was her only son and after the two girls, she and Tom had so desperately wanted a son, so they gave it one more go and along came the most beautiful baby boy ever, and to this day June still idolised him.

"Can I get you a cuppa while you're here, Meg?"

"No thanks, Mum, I was literally just passing so thought I'd just make sure you're OK." Meghan only lived a few streets away from June, which was nice for all of them as Jane was busy with her career in London and Paul lived thirty miles away.

"I've got to get Chris's stuff ready for uni." June's grandson started his university course in a few weeks' time and preparations for his move were well under way. Meghan had another child, Samantha, who was going to go back to the sixth form soon.

It was all go in Meghan's household, where she and her husband David were continually busy, both working - although Meghan part-time - but there were always things to be done. Meghan was amazing at what she did in keeping everybody happy, but June knew that sometimes the strain took it out of her daughter and it upset her sometimes to see Meghan so tired, but not being able to have some time to relax. It didn't seem to be so frenzied when June was bringing up her family: there didn't seem to be so many pressures for families back then, she wondered if all this progress was such a great thing sometimes.

"OK then, Mum, I'll be off now but I'll either

pop in or phone you to let you know the date of the get-together. I'll speak to the other two tonight."

"OK darling, thanks for popping in, sorry I gave you a scare being in the attic and not hearing the door. Love you." She kissed her daughter on the cheek and gave her a hug. Meg was such a lovely soul, but then so were the other two; she was an incredibly lucky Mum.

Once Meghan had left, June resumed her thought pattern about Tom, except this time it involved the nonsense that Mr James had come out with. She thought it was such a load of old rubbish but - and this was the thing - she was free to try something mad and crazy, why not give it a go? Sure, she would feel stupid but who was to see? If it did not work, she was unsure what she would do. Go and see Mr James? No. She decided she would just put it down to weirdness in life and hopefully never bump into him again. Would she report him for approaching a vulnerable widow? She knew she should, but could she really be bothered to fight? Should she go to the police? Too dramatic. No, she would just have to act like it never happened. But it brought her back to why he would have said what he did, what did he have to gain? It was this thought that made her decide to give it a go. It would be tonight.

CHAPTER 2

It was ten o'clock on Friday night and June had spent the evening watching television. She wanted to go to bed, as her eyes felt heavy. The thing about age was she always seemed to feel tired, no matter how much rest she had. She tried to avoid the "nanny naps" that her children always used to make fun of their father for: Tom would sit down to read in the afternoon but before he even got to turn a page he would nod off. It was nothing like the young Tom, who could go for days with hardly any sleep and still have boundless energy to play with the children after work or take June out for a meal. He hardly ever missed a day's work. Tom loved his job as a carpenter. He was never without work, often being called back to places that he had worked at previously and constantly had a diary full of work, both for companies and private customers alike. He made a success of the business, working alongside Joe, his partner. June adored Joe and his wife Shirley, who was a few years older than June and was one of the sweetest people she had met. They had one child, who used to come over with them and play with her children. June asked Shirley one day about whether they wanted more children, but Shirley said that sadly, they were unable to have any more and June was always touched by how lovely Shirley was each time June announced a pregnancy.

June got up to go and get the candle she had under the sink but never used, all the time questioning her own actions. This all felt very strange and she wondered how batty her children would say she was, even contemplating doing this, but there were some things that were between Tom and her and nothing to do with the children: this private experiment was one such thing. She lit the candle and placed it on the mantlepiece, taking the record from its sleeve and putting it on the record player, which she and Tom had kept, despite her children's protestations about getting an updated player. The record player and radio were more than sufficient for her and Tom; she didn't need the new-fangled devices that her children wanted them to have, they were fine with their old player. They had not used it for a long time though and June hoped it was still working. She placed the record on the turntable and switched it on. It gave a quick buzz and the power light glowed green.

Before she switched off the lights, she gave herself a check in the mirror. She looked tidy and acceptable and gave little importance to Mr James's claim that her physical presence would change. That was an impossibility, surely.

She had one last look around the room and said to herself, "You're mad, doing this," then switched off the light. She made her way over to the record player and lifted the needle. The turntable began to turn, she placed the needle at the start of the record and stood absolutely still, closing her eyes. The beautiful song began, memories of a young Tom and her came flooding back and her eyes began to fill with tears. She felt desperate to open her eyes, to put a stop to this stupidity for fear of ever being found out that she had indulged in something so ridiculous. She wanted to stop this now: she would, she would open her eyes now and stop this nonsense.

Instead, she whispered softly "Tom." It was then, at that moment, at that doubt, at that impossibility in her mind - she heard it: she heard it as clear as crystal. She heard Tom. She heard him say, "June," and her heart stopped. She squeezed her eyes more tightly shut as she didn't even think the voice she had heard was real. Her imagination, together with the music and the candlelight, all going to serve toward making her *think* she had heard him, but then she heard him again.

"Open your eyes, June."

She did and what she saw both frightened her and made her so happy - more than anything she was confused at what she was seeing. There, stood across the room, was Tom, not the Tom that she had last seen, but a twenty-three-year-old Tom, the age he was when they had met, just like Mr James had said.

"Tom!" was all she could say. They both stood rooted to their respective spots, both too scared to move, should they break this spell.

"Tom," she began, "I don't understand. I'm totally confused. How is this happening?"

"Don't question it, June. I'm here because what you and I had was special. I want to spend these two weeks with you and treasure every moment. I love you so much, Beanie," he said, using the nickname he had given her because he thought she was always on the go when they were young. He had said she was like a little jumping-bean; the name had stuck and been affectionately lengthened.

"God, Tom, I love you too, so very much. You are so handsome though, so young, I'm an old wreck."

"No, you're not June. Take a look in the

mirror."

June turned round to look in the mirror and was totally shocked by the reflection staring back at her. She was speechless at what she saw - a beautiful young woman with long flowing hair, perfect skin, full lips and the most amazing figure that was slim and supple underneath the clothes she was wearing, clothes that had been on a seventy-four-year-old woman but which now hung over the small frame of a twenty-year-old girl. Even though June was shocked at the reflection, she knew it was herself and recognised the June she saw. Tom started to walk across the room and came close to her from behind, they shared a reflection, two young people in love and wanting to be together.

Tom placed his hands on her waist and slowly bent to kiss her neck. All the desire June had felt for him when they were young came rushing back, she swung round and eagerly found his lips with hers, they kissed long and hard and already June was moaning with desire for her husband. Tom began to undress her and to touch her, she pulled him close.

"Shall we go to bed?" she asked him, shocked at her overwhelming desire.

"Oh yes my darling," he said breathlessly and she took his hand, taking him up the stairs to their bedroom. Once inside, they fell on the bed, June began to undo his shirt and rub her hands on his beautiful chest. She put her lips against it and licked his skin. They continued to kiss while they both got undressed and when they were naked, he lay on top of her, kissing her lips and neck and touching her everywhere. She did the same to him, marvelling at the feel of his body and the way his smell made her want to have him inside her. He entered her and they began to feel that amazing dizzy feeling that only making love can give. Tom came and so did June and they were both in paradise. When they were finished, they lay naked together, both of their bodies sweating and still warm with desire. Tom kissed her again.

"I love you, June" and she lay in his arms never wanting to let go of him again.

"Tom?" she said.

"Yes, my darling" he replied.

"Tom, what is this all about? I'm really confused, is it a dream?"

"No, my darling, it's not a dream but you can't ask for an explanation, it just is and we must not question it too much."

"But..." June began but Tom put his finger on her lips.

"No June, I have no answers. I only know we have to take it and just accept it without explanation," and he kissed her again. They both felt desire welling up again, it was very strange to feel so energised for June that she wanted to make love again, but she remembered she was a twenty-year-old girl and all that came with that. She felt her hair, long and thick, she looked down at her body, at the smooth skin and supple thighs and legs, even her feet were dainty and pretty. They started to kiss again and before long Tom was inside her for another journey into pleasure. They both fell asleep, relaxed and in a state of bliss as they felt themselves next to each other.

They awoke early, June looked at the clock, it said six-thirty and for a split second, marvelled at the lucidity of last night's dream, but then she felt Tom's body against hers and the reality of him being here struck her with equal force as it did last night. She leant over, her hair falling on his face and kissed him, he opened his eyes and smiled, he touched her cheek and said, "Good morning, my darling, I love you so much."

June's heart skipped a beat as she replied, "I love you too Tom. I don't know what this is or where it came from but we're so lucky to have it, I'm not going to waste a minute." He looked at her and felt desire washing over him again. He pulled her to him, and they made glorious love again. Afterwards, June got in the shower, washing every inch of her wonderful young body, she forgot how it felt to be able to move quickly and be pain free. Her seventy-four-year-old joints weren't great at moving quickly or with ease, so she was amazed at how much she felt like she was walking on air in her twenty-year-old frame. She didn't want to be too long in the shower, as she didn't want to waste too much time away from Tom. She did think there were so many questions which would never be answered so she needed to just make the most of this time and not search for answers. She wondered last night if Tom would actually get tired, if he was some sort of spirit but, so far, he seemed to have all the same needs as she did, including being hungry as he had asked her cheekily what was for breakfast.

When she got out of the shower, she dried herself and stood looking in the full-length mirror at her reflection, she turned to look at her neat, pert little bottom and put her hands over her breasts which were also pert and a perfect size, as Tom always used to say. She realised she was actually incredibly beautiful and "quite the babe", as their granddaughter

Samantha would say. As she was coming out of the bathroom, Tom was approaching, naked, holding the towel she had given him. He pulled her to him and kissed her but took hold of her arm and gently pulled her along. He stepped into the shower and pulled her in toward him, she didn't care that she had already showered. He switched on the water, and it poured over both of them. This was something they had never done when they were young, to shower together, and she was happy to be able to do it now. Tom put some soap on his hands and turned her so her back was facing him, he began to soap the front of her body, over her breasts and down over her tummy. She moaned at the electricity of his touch and turned to face him, needing to feel his lips on hers, they kissed, and she pushed her body onto his. They made love in the shower and afterwards, dried each other with the towels.

Tom put the clothes back on that he had been wearing but June threw on something that was not even remotely fun and young. She had plenty of T-shirts, although her underwear was not only rather sensible but also far too big. It would have to do until she could buy some younger underwear, she was fine to walk around the house bra-less and she knew Tom would be more than happy with this. She put a T-shirt on and some leggings, she turned the leggings up to show off more of her slim, smooth legs and went downstairs, where Tom was already sitting at the table looking out into the garden.

June put the kettle on. "What are you thinking, Tom?"

"I'm thinking how strange it is that I know that garden so well, how weird all of this is. I haven't got a clue how I got here or who made it possible but all I know is it's the most incredible feeling in the world, to be with you. How are our children, June? I won't be able to see them, but I know them. I may have come back twenty-three years old, but I left this world at seventy-seven and remember everything I left."

"The children are well, but obviously still hurting at losing their Dad. Jane has gone back to London and Meg's just up the road so I'm sure I'll see plenty of her. Paul took it hard and has withdrawn into his own world a bit, but I'm seeing them all soon, I'll get some photos. Meg mentioned a get-together before Chris goes off to university but I won't be staying, I can't be without you Tom, not even for one evening. This is a God-given gift and I don't want to waste it."

"I understand, sweetheart. I want these last moments with you too, so our children will have to wait for overnighters for a couple of weeks." They both smiled, knowing that as ever, they both felt the same way. June made a lovely breakfast of egg on toast for them both and put some croissants in the oven to heat. Again, in her mind she thought that she really didn't know if Tom would need food, but he seemed to be just like any other person while he was with her. June cleared up the breakfast things while Tom sat and watched her, occasionally grabbing her arm to pull her to him to kiss her, marvelling at how beautiful she was.

"What shall we do now, Tom?"

"Let's go into the attic and dig out those old records. After all we've only got a couple of hours left, we might as well enjoy it."

June felt sad at the prospect of having to say goodbye to her husband.

"OK," she replied, "Let's go and get them."

June went back into the attic for the second time in two days, but this time Tom came up there with her. He saw all the boxes he had packed away over the years and went over to the box marked "Records" – *ironically*, thought June, *where all this began*.

"Let's take the lot down."

"That'll be too heavy, Tom."

"Well, you go down and wait at the bottom and I'll pass a few at a time."

June waited at the bottom while Tom passed them, taking them through to their bedroom and putting them on the bed. There were about fifty in total, so this took some time, eating into their time together, which June was conscious of. When they had them all, they took them downstairs to their old record player. The first one Tom put on was their Dusty Springfield album. Tom turned the volume up. He grabbed her hand and whirled her around. They danced apart, together and laughed like children. June was amazed at the suppleness of her young body, the way she could bend and sway like she used to. The next song to come on was slow and soulful. Tom took her in his arms and together they swayed to the beautiful song.

"June, this feels wonderful." She felt his breath against her hair, at that moment she knew what paradise was. As the song came to an end, Tom put his forehead against June's. She knew he didn't want to let her go; she didn't want him to. The next few songs were dance songs: they jumped, they span, they even did a head over heels (impressing June with her new-found flexibility even more) until they were both breathless and sweating. Both laughing, they flopped onto the settee. There was one final song that Tom wanted to play. He put it on the record player and Bob Dylan's "I Want You" blared out. Tom had always mimed this song to June when they were young - he was quite a Dylan fan back then - *obviously still was, going by today*, thought June. He stood doing his best Dylan impression and miming the words to June. He pulled her up and to him and they danced together to the rest of the song. June had had such a fantastic morning, she looked at the clock on the mantlepiece: they had less than an hour left. She was intrigued; would he just disappear in a puff of smoke, would he gradually disappear, how would this go? More importantly, would he come back tonight?

"Tom, look at the time," she said.

"I know, darling. I wonder what we can do in that time?" he asked with a mischievous look on his face. These two people were in their little conspiratorial world and they were having so much fun in their own little bubble, blocking all others out temporarily. June never thought she'd ever experience such wonderful times again after losing Tom but for whatever reason, some powers greater than we know deemed her worthy of such a great reward as she was experiencing now.

"I don't know, Tom, what *can* we do?" she said, smiling back with a coquettish little slant to her head. She got up and started to run upstairs. He followed swiftly, knowing the pleasure that they were about to experience one last time today. Afterwards, June looked at the clock: their time today was nearly at an end.

"Tom…"

He stopped her. "I know darling. But there's tomorrow."

A silent tear started to fall down her face, she was about to lose him all over again, but what had happened was better than never having him again at all. He jumped up and dressed, he told her to go and shower if she wanted, but she didn't want to wash his smell off her. She sat staring at him, touching his hair. She put her hand down to find his: it wasn't there... he had gone and she cried to have him back.

It took a while for June to get up and compose herself for the rest of the day. What she noticed first was the aches as she climbed out of bed, she looked down at herself and the body she had become more familiar with had returned. Her skin was patchy and veined, she was still slim but nothing like her twenty-year-old self. She didn't mind. She was happy in her own skin at seventy-four. Being twenty had been fantastic but only because she could be young again with Tom; on her own she didn't care. She stood up and looked in the mirror, took some different clothes from the wardrobe and got dressed. She could smell Tom on her, this was all she needed for the rest of the day until tonight, when she could be with him again. June assumed it would work again, mad as it was. It had worked once so there was no reason to doubt Mr James's assurance. June went downstairs to make lunch. When the phone rang, she answered it to hear Meghan's voice.

"Hello Mum, all OK with you?"

"Yes Meg, how are you, sweetheart? Chris ready for uni yet?"

"Ha-ha, you're joking aren't you, Mum? He's made a new list as long as your arm which for some reason, includes fourteen Pot Noodles, despite the fact we've bought him new cookware and crockery and he's given me his assurance that he'll be eating healthily. He said all these Pot Noodles are just 'for emergencies'."

June laughed at the ongoing battle between mother and son about nutrition, one she remembers well from her days bringing up Paul, who, when he turned into a teenager, seemed to develop some sort of phobia of vegetables.

"Oh dear, Meg. Good luck with the food debate," laughed June.

"Anyway, Mum, why I'm ringing is that I've

managed to nab Jane and Paul next weekend and I thought as Chris is going to uni the week after, it'd be an excellent time to get together for the family before he goes. The weather's meant to be glorious, so David is going to don his pinny and barbecue."

"That's lovely Meg. I'll get a taxi."

"Don't be silly, Mum. I'll pick you up Saturday at, shall we say eleven?" June did a quick calculation of time in her head and decided that if she could be home by seven, she could still get some quality time with Tom.

"Yes, that'll be great," June replied eventually.

"What are you up to this weekend Mum? You can come over and stay if you like."

June knew that her weekend was going to be busy, but if she dared tell her children why, they would think she was mad. "I'm fine Meg. To be honest, I'm looking forward to a bit of 'me' time. I think I'll spoil myself with some very boring TV and just relax. I want some time alone after all that's happened. It seems to have been non-stop since we lost your Dad. I'd like some time alone to think about him."

"That's what I'm worried about, Mum, that you'll just sit and think and be very morose or depressed, even. I think you ought to be where people can take your mind off things and the kids would love to see you."

June's guilt was immense. "I know, Meg, I will come over to stay soon, I promise, but for now I'm really fine to be on my own, you needn't worry. In fact, the memories are all happy ones, you wouldn't believe how happy your Dad still makes me feel, even now." June knew this was not a lie but could not even begin to explain. Firstly, she would negate any further visits from Tom and secondly, Meghan would think she had lost her marbles completely.

"OK, Mum, if you're sure. I'll probably see you in the week at some point but if not, I'll pick you up Saturday at eleven."

"OK, sweetheart, bye for now and say hello to everyone for me. Love you."

"Love you too, Mum. Bye."

June was happy to end the call. She hated lying to her children. She had only ever done it once or twice, but this was very necessary, very necessary indeed and her mind once again turned to Tom.

It was two o'clock on Saturday afternoon and June took the record out of its sleeve, placed it on the turntable, switched the record player on and put the needle across. She stood back and closed her eyes, wondering if it would really happen again. She still felt very strange doing this, because it wasn't really anything that should be done in normality, but what had happened last night was definitely not any normality she had ever known. As she stood there, hands clasped and eyes tightly shut she heard the familiar voice of yesterday.

"Hello, Beanie."

She opened her eyes and saw Tom standing there again and jumped into his arms, something she was amazed she could do with such grace and ease, they kissed passionately and laughed together at the joy being together brought them. June then left his arms to run to the mirror and saw the beautiful girl with the long shiny hair looking back at her. She was almost as amazed as yesterday at the transformation into her twenty-year-old self that this magical experience brought her.

"Yes Beanie, you're still as beautiful at twenty as you are at seventy-four."

"You too Tom. Handsome that is. Shall I get us some tea?"

"Yes, that sounds like a good idea... afterwards."

With that, he took her hand, kissed her again and worked his way down to her neck. She felt desire rising in her again and he took her hand, leading her up the stairs to their bed and they made love. Afterwards they lay together naked, Tom stroking her hair and back, both were in paradise once again.

"Tom?" she asked.

"Yes darling?"

"This is all so odd, isn't it?"

"Yes, it is but I'm not going to question it June, I'm scared that if we question it too much it'll go... we'll break the spell or something."

"I know what you mean Tom, but I mean, who sent you, what happens before you get here?"

"I haven't got a clue June, I just find myself here, I find myself at twenty-something and here with you. The bits in between I have no memory of, it's difficult to explain, I know nothing and then I'm just here. Who told you how to do this?"

"It was really strange, I had a visit from Mr James, the funeral director, and he told me we were genuine soulmates and when that happens, and it's rare, the couple are allowed this experience of two extra weeks together, but as their young selves. He said obviously no one else could share the secret, that it would come to an end if I ever tried to tell anybody and they'd think I was bonkers anyway, but I wouldn't really want to. I just want every moment to be with just you and I so that we can cherish these two weeks."

"I agree, we get twelve hours together each day, let's just enjoy it for what it is. Now Beanie, what about that tea?"

"Yep, come on then."

They both got up, June put a T-shirt on with her panties, Tom just put his trousers back on and they went downstairs into the kitchen. They drank their tea and spoke about the children, who strangely, wouldn't have even been born yet. She told him how they were after losing him and how she was more worried about Paul than the girls.

"Oh June, you always worried more about him. Just make sure you keep an eye on him. I know how badly he suffered after the divorce but at least they never had any children; he could make a clean break. I'm sure he'll meet someone eventually who will make him want to settle down again but until then, all you can do is be there. He's a grown man after all."

"I know, Tom. I'll be seeing him next weekend: Meg's having a barbecue."

"That'll be nice for you. Hopefully not a late one as I think you've got a date with a handsome young man when you get home."

June laughed, "Definitely not too late - it's a date I intend to keep." She mouthed a kiss at him.

"Now young lady, I noticed your grass is looking a bit long so I thought I'd give it a mow and tidy the garden a bit... if you don't mind of course."

June was surprised at this; she'd never really thought about either of them going outside. "But Tom, supposing Fran sees you?"

"And? You just say you got a gardener in."

"Yes, I suppose so." June was grateful that their house was quite far away from Fran's and there was nothing on the other side, so thought there wouldn't be any harm in letting Tom do some gardening. He had always loved the garden, even when they were young.

"Alright then, but I won't be able to come

outside. I'll sit in the conservatory with the door open and we can talk. I'll watch you mow the lawn but only if you promise to keep your shirt off."

"Sounds like a deal, Beanie. Then you can cook us a nice meal later, we can have some wine and then find something to do." He came up behind June where she was sitting at the table and started to rub her shoulders. She knew after supper they would go to bed and that's probably where they would stay until Tom went.

June went to the conservatory and sat facing the garden, watching Tom get the lawnmower from the shed. She loved watching him do this familiar task, it made her feel they were a couple again. She couldn't take her eyes off him while he mowed, his beautiful back and chest glistening with sweat. Her mind wandered to what she would do for tea, they always enjoyed their meals together, opting to stay in for meals as they got older, rather than go out. June was an amazing cook, and they always made a proper occasion of eating dinner - always at the dining table and always with a glass or two of wine. She decided upon lasagne, she had some mince in the freezer and Tom had always loved her lasagne, she would serve it with salad and a nice bottle of Merlot that had been in their wine rack since before Tom passed away. She did not really drink alone; wine had always been a shared pleasure with Tom and that was taken away when he died.

She thought about his death, how quickly it had happened and how unexpected it had been. Although he was in his seventies, Tom had always seemed in such good health. They had decided to go out one day, to randomly and spontaneously go to the seaside. They hadn't been for years and thought how nice it would be to visit the coast, have a fish and chip supper and they may even find a little hotel somewhere and stay over until the next day. They packed a few things in a backpack, looked up train times and booked a taxi. When they had got up the next day, they were ready and waiting for the taxi that was picking them up at 10 am. Tom seemed fine; together they both got in the taxi and arrived at the station well in time for their train. Once on the platform, Tom had said he felt a little strange: June noticed he was sweating and thought it was just the warm day taking it out of him. She spotted a kiosk on the opposite platform and with plenty of time until their train, said she would go and get him a bottle of water, which he agreed would be nice. She walked up the stairs and across the bridge over the track, down the other side and began to walk toward the kiosk. She glanced over at Tom, who she had left sitting on the bench, but was alarmed to see he had fallen to one side. She called out his name and forgot all about the water: she had to get back to Tom to find out what was wrong. She ran quickly across the bridge and down to the platform, running to the end where they had been sitting. By this time two or three people were watching her as she got to her beloved husband, who had slumped over. He was grey and lifeless. She screamed his name, someone called an ambulance, the rest was a haze. The ambulance arrived, they gave him CPR, put him in the ambulance and connected him to machines. When they got to the hospital he was rushed into Resus. June was held back and told to wait for a doctor. One eventually came and she knew by his face and the way he started his sentence.

"Mrs Reader..." June knew: she knew her precious husband was dead. It had been a massive heart attack, very quick, very sudden and Tom was gone, in what felt like the blink of an eye, he had been dead in the ambulance, she found out. Her eyes filled with tears at not only the thought of losing her beloved husband, but also at having to tell the children their father was dead.

When she did, the girls had cried, her grandchildren cried into Meghan's shoulder as she hugged them tightly and Paul put both his hands over his face and, as she watched his shoulders shake, knew that tears would be running down his face. She felt selfish now at having this time with their father when they could not, but knew that it was something that their marriage and all its successes had earnt them. They were a team, a partnership, they belonged together. Their children had their own lives to forge and mould, she and Tom had spent their lives as one and this was their reward, just two more weeks of twelve hours a day.

This brought her back to the present, where Tom was still happily mowing the lawn. He looked at her and did a little kiss. June hoped that Fran hadn't seen the fact that her young gardener seemed very friendly with an old lady like June; this thought made her smile. She looked down at her long legs, out straight and supported by a footstool: *they really were great legs*, she thought. She looked at her watch: plenty of time yet. Tom continued to tend the garden as she sat watching and occasionally getting up to get them both a glass of water or a biscuit. He finished the lawn and June called him into the conservatory to let him know she'd be putting dinner on soon and asked whether he wanted a shower.

"You can carry on the garden tomorrow, Tom."

"Yes, OK Beanie, I'll just put the mower away." He went outside, put the mower in the shed and came in.

"So, I'm having a shower."

"That's fine, Tom. I'll start tea."

"Really Beanie? That's a bit cruel."

"Why? What's cruel?"

"Well," he replied trying to reach a part of his back, "I've got this bit here, just up a bit, that no matter how hard I try, I just can't reach to wash."

"So? What do you want me to do about it?" June asked mischievously.

"I wondered if you knew anyone that could come up and wash it for me?"

June laughed and kissed him, "I think I do, yes."

They went upstairs together and showered. They never intended to make love again, but the touch of each other's bodies meant their desire was too strong.

After their shower they came back down and June began to prepare tea. Tom went into the lounge and began to play music again. He loved music, as did June, and they shared the same taste. She heard Dylan blaring out yet again and then he moved on to Al Green. June loved the sultry soulful sound of Al Green - perfect music for a perfect evening. June put the lasagne in the oven, poured them both a glass of wine and joined Tom in the lounge, where she sat next to him listening to the music.

When the lasagne had cooked, June served it with salad and they brought their wine to the dining table, where they sat eating their food.

"Mmmm, delicious Beanie. You do make a fine meal."

"Thank you darling, glad you're enjoying it."

It was already eight o'clock, the time seemed

to go so fast, having Tom with her. They drank the bottle of Merlot with their dinner and spoke about old times, about when they met.

"I had my eye on you from the start, Beanie, as soon as you walked into Dad's shop." Tom usually helped his Dad in his hardware shop on Saturdays. He enjoyed spending the time with his father and meeting all the people that came into the shop. On this particular day, a man came in with his daughter. She was absolutely gorgeous, Tom thought, and it was a pleasant change to see a young woman come into the shop: it was usually middle-aged men, tasked with redecorating the home and asking advice about brushes or drills or some such very unglamorous object, but today the shop had a bit of glamour when this beautiful young woman came in. Tom rushed over to help them, smiling broadly at the young woman and adopting a serious look and tone for her father, wanting to impress the girl with his great knowledge about paintbrushes or some such. June's Dad knew what he was looking for thank goodness. Tom could just go and get it and take the money. As they left, he said a loud goodbye to them both. June looked round and smiled, with a look in her eyes that told Tom the attraction was mutual.

They had met up again on a night out when they both went to the same dance hall. He caught sight of her and immediately left his group of friends to go over and introduce himself. They spent the evening talking and dancing. At the end of the night, Tom asked her on a date and the rest, as they say, is history.

Their date was a meal in a nearby restaurant. It was either that or the cinema, but June wanted to get to know Tom, which watching a film would not help her do. After that, they had many more dates and each time was better than the last until it came to that time of meeting the parents. Both June and Tom knew at an early stage this relationship was going to be a serious one. It was everything they could want: shared interests, a friendship, a partnership and before too long, a passionate love. June was twenty when they met, Tom twenty-three. When June was twenty-one, he proposed, she immediately accepted and he made the visit to ask her father for her hand in marriage. Both sets of parents were delighted, they both liked their offspring's choice of marriage partner, which was always a bonus for any young couple.

June and Tom, feeling the warmth of the Merlot, both spoke about their wedding day, about the best man, Tom's brother Eddie, now sadly dead, about the bridesmaids, about the argument between Eddie and Sylvie, his French wife, who he'd met on a night out in London. The argument was because Eddie was having far too good a time with her best friend Nina. Although Eddie was the perpetual flirt, he never meant any harm, but Sylvie never quite got used to how harmless Eddie's flirting was. The irony of this was that when he lost Sylvie prematurely to breast cancer when she was only forty-six, something went out in him.

He no longer seemed to enjoy life, he became more and more isolated from everyone until he too died prematurely at just fifty-three, after being diagnosed with a fierce late-stage brain tumour, which had only shown itself in increased headaches and a period of dizziness. Eddie's speech began to slur slightly and it was this that prompted him to go for tests, where they found the shocking discovery. He was dead within twelve weeks of the diagnosis, deteriorating physically and mentally very rapidly. Eddie's death hit Tom very badly, he went into a bout of depression at losing his big brother. At three years older, Eddie had always taken care of him and Tom missed him terribly, but he had June to cradle him in her arms and let him cry the tears that the pain of losing his brother and best friend brought.

June looked at her watch, it was 10 pm and she had not even washed the dishes. They did this together, Tom insisting on interrupting all the time by grabbing her from behind and kissing her hair. They laughed and had fun washing up together, they made coffee and sat looking into each other's eyes as they spoke gently and quietly about how lucky they were to get this time together. Tom eventually took her hand and they went upstairs, where they made love and lay together. June was determined not to go to sleep as she lay on Tom's chest, but she couldn't help shutting her eyes. When she opened them again Tom was gone, she looked at the clock, it was 6 am, he had been gone four hours. She put her face on his pillow and fell asleep again. She dreamt of him because she wanted him back.

June woke up and looked at the clock, it was 8 am. Time to get up, shower and get to the shops; she wanted to get a nice steak for them to have for dinner tonight. She had planned for him to visit at midday, so it did not leave her long. June was ready to leave by nine and walked the short distance into town, where she would go into her usual butchers and get the steaks. As she walked into the shop, she was greeted warmly by Colin - he had been their butcher for many years now. Colin knew Tom had passed away and he expressed his condolences.

"Thank you, Colin, that's very kind of you."

"How are you in yourself, Mrs Reader? You know I'll always deliver if you have an order. Just phone and we'll bring it to you the same day."

"Thanks, I might take you up on that, but for now I'd just like a couple of nice steaks."

"Of course." Colin wrapped two large rump steaks.

"*Tom will like those,*" thought June.

"Having company?" Colin asked.

"Yes, an old friend is coming over to talk about old times," June said, not a million miles from the truth.

"Well, enjoy. They're good cuts."

"Thanks Colin, take care and I'll phone if I need to order anything."

"Of course. Take one of our cards on the counter - it has the phone number on it."

June took a card and left. She walked down

the High Street to a clothes shop. She really needed some clothes to wear when Tom came, as her seventy-four-year-old wardrobe wasn't too great for a twenty-year-old. She went into the shop and started to look at the array of items. She spotted a couple of really pretty dresses which were a lot shorter than she would currently wear. She picked both up in a size eight, which was her twenty-year-old size. She felt very out of place, looking at these clothes in her present body, but she pictured what they would look like on her while Tom was there. She also bought some fancy underwear and strappy sandals, getting to the till and saying, "For my granddaughter" to the assistant, as she felt she needed to explain.

The assistant smiled and said, "These are all lovely, I'm sure she'll be very pleased."

On the way back, June stopped at a chemist and asked an assistant what a good perfume for a young woman would be. The assistant pointed to a few.

"Which one would you wear?" June asked.

"Oh, definitely this one," she said, picking up a bottle priced at £40.

"I'll take that please," said June, thinking that it was a bit pricey, but she wanted a special perfume for this time with Tom.

When June got home, she knew it would be useless to try the dresses on, she would wait until they fitted and suited her young body. She looked at her watch, it was already eleven o'clock. She would have a cup of tea and tidy up a bit, then put their song on. As she began to get the vacuum out, the doorbell rang, she answered the door to see Fran.

"Hi June, got time for a cuppa?"

June didn't know what to say to put Fran off, except, "Well, I was just about to tidy up."

"I won't stop long," she said, undeterred.

"Yes, sure. Come in."

June put the kettle on, hoping this would be a quick visit. Fran sat at the table and saw the bags from the clothes shop.

"Been treating yourself, June?" she asked.

"Yes, I thought why not, I've got a barbecue

at Meghan's next Saturday so I thought I'd get something nice to wear," she said, trying to be nonchalant and hoping Fran would change the subject.

"Let's have a look," Fran said, thinking June would be happy to share her purchases.

"Oh, in a minute. I'm parched, let's have this tea." June hoped that would be enough to make Fran forget about the bags.

"So, how have you been?" Fran asked, concerned. She thought June seemed a lot better than their last meeting on the day of the funeral.

"Yes, I've been good, thanks Fran. I'm getting used to being on my own."

"I'll say," said Fran, "I walked past your house yesterday morning when I walked the dog. All I could hear was music, you had a trip down memory lane, didn't you?"

"Er, yes. Those songs remind me of Tom, they were all his favourites."

Fran laughed. "It sounded like you were having a party," she said, "Grieving is a funny thing. If playing loud music helps you, June, then you do it."

"It does help, to be honest."

Fran started to tell June all about her visit to the hospital. June continually looked at the clock above Fran's head.

"Are you expecting someone, June? You keep looking at the time." Fran sensed June was distracted.

"No, no, sorry. I was just hoping to get the housework done so that I can have the rest of the day."

"It's only ten to twelve, I'll leave you in peace then and you can carry on." Fran felt rather like she was being hurried out, but just assumed June wanted to be alone with her thoughts.

"Thanks for popping in Fran, I'll see you soon."

As she closed the front door, she realised she had no interest in housework, she just wanted to see Tom, so she immediately went into the lounge and put their record on. She stood with her eyes closed until she heard his familiar voice.

"Hello, Beanie."

She opened her eyes and saw her lovely husband standing there. She looked in the mirror to check her reflection and saw the twenty-year-old June looking back at her. They hurried toward each other and kissed. He tasted so good, and she melted into his arms.

"I miss you when you're not here Tom."

"I know, darling, but I'm here now."

June suddenly remembered her dresses: she ran into the kitchen and grabbed the bags.

"Stay there, Tom, I've bought some new clothes and I want to put them on for you."

"OK, Beanie, give me a fashion show, gorgeous girl."

She took the bags upstairs and hurriedly took off the clothes she was wearing that hung from her girl's frame, she hated them on her young body. She put the underwear on first and was amazed how pretty she looked, then she put on one of the dresses. It was floral and had a ruffle round the neckline, which was cut exceptionally low to expose her smooth cleavage. She put the sandals on and looked at herself in the mirror, she grabbed a hair band and tied her long hair up in a ponytail. As she came down the stairs, she saw Tom sitting in the lounge and went in, standing in front of him. She gave him a twirl.

"Wow, Beanie, you look amazing. What a beautiful dress, did you choose it?"

"Yes, darling, I got it for your visit today and I also got you some steak for later. I thought we'd have a lovely candlelit meal tonight."

"Steak?" he said, licking his lips. "You're spoiling me."

"I want to spoil you." She looked at him cheekily then lifted her dress to reveal the new underwear. "Look, I got these to wear for you too."

He took her hand and guided her to sit next to him.

"You know how to make me happy, don't you, Beanie?" and he kissed her, sliding his hand up her dress. She moaned with pleasure and he pulled her down onto the floor where they made love. It had been a long time since they had made love on a floor, but the marvels of youth are that there are no rules for passion; there certainly never were for them when they were young. Afterwards they sat together on the sofa, holding each other for a long time. June jumped at the phone when it rang. She looked at Tom, unsure what to do. Should she answer it? Tom said leave it for the answerphone to pick up, which they did. It was their son Paul. "Hi, Mum, it's Paul. Just a quick message to say if you're in today, I'm in the area and could pop in to see you. No worries if you're not in, I'll give you a knock. It should be about four."

June and Tom knew they could not possibly answer the door, so would have to pretend not to be in. She would feel awful ignoring Paul but there was no other option. They decided to spend the time until Paul arrived watching their favourite film on DVD, cuddled up on the sofa, taking a break to make a pot of tea and eat biscuits. At half-past three they went upstairs to the bedroom and sat on the bed talking about Paul. They both worried about him and felt sad that they could not see him as a couple, but when your Mum and Dad find themselves in a situation where they are much younger than you, it really cannot be done. It was ten past four when the doorbell rang. They sat silently and guiltily ignoring their own son. The bell rang again and she heard Paul walk over the gravel to look up at the window. Then she heard Fran's voice who had just got back from walking the dog.

"Hello Paul, how are you?"

"Hello Fran, yes, I'm fine thanks. I was just passing and thought I'd pop in and see Mum but she's not in."

"Oh, she was in earlier. She didn't say anything at the time about going out."

"Do you think she's OK?" he asked.

June looked at Tom with a fearful look, she did not know what to do and dreaded this turning into a big thing.

"To be honest Paul, she seemed absolutely fine when I saw her, but she was a bit distracted. She's probably just gone for a walk or something, as she did say she was enjoying her own company, that it gave her a chance to think about your Dad." June silently thanked Fran for the reassurance she had given Paul.

"Yes, you're right. She and Dad did like to walk so she's probably just retracing their old steps. I'll call her later and if I don't get a reply, I'll ask Meg to pop round - she has a key."

"That's a good idea. It is difficult but I'm sure she's fine."

Paul got into his car and drove off. June knew that when he called later, she would have to answer the phone.

They both went downstairs and sat in the conservatory, looking through old photos and talking about their courting days until the phone rang. June answered it and lowered her voice an octave as she said hello to Paul.

"Hi Mum, I came round earlier but you

weren't in."

"Oh, sorry darling, I decided to go for a walk."

"Exactly what Fran said. Did you have a nice time?"

"Yes, I went to a few of the places Dad and I used to go and thought of him and our times together."

"That's nice."

"So, how are you, Paul?"

"Good Mum, I'm taking a break from dating and having some quality time with me, myself and I. I think I've been trying to run away from the fact that I'm single now." June was pleased to hear Paul sound so sensible; she knew it wasn't easy for him to be on his own, but she thought if he was to stand a chance of another relationship, he had to allow himself to get over his marriage.

"That's good to hear Paul, I'm proud of you, always have been. I can't wait to see you on Saturday at Meg's barbecue."

"Yes, can't wait to see you Mum. See you

Saturday. Love you."

When she hung up the phone she turned to Tom. "He's fine Tom. Sounds really well in fact."

"That's good, he'll always be our little boy, eh Beanie?"

"He sure will. Anyway, come on you, I need to marinade a steak, you wait until you see the monster I got you."

"Can we have another party after tea Beanie? After all, you did buy a new dress and it is quite sexy, so I need to see you dance."

"Yes, my darling, let's do that and I'm glad you like the dress, although it felt very weird an old biddy like me buying it for myself. This whole thing messes terribly with your head."

"I know, but I'm loving it, are you?"

"It's paradise, Tom." And she kissed him tenderly.

They ate their meal. Tom was impressed with his steak. June certainly knew how to cook. He had been an incredibly lucky man since he met her: she had brought so much into his life, all of it happy. They had three lovely children and although money had been tight at times, having a partner who pulled with you in the same direction and did not send any guilt your way over money was always a blessing. Tom and June washed up together, again with the same happy abandonment that made even this mundane task fun. When they had finished, they took another bottle of Merlot and their glasses into the lounge and Tom put The Seekers on: "I'll Never Find Another You", a song he devoted to June at the time. He worked through the music, they both danced and drank wine until their heads were spinning. When Dusty came on with a slow song, they danced together holding each other tight, their young bodies lithe and supple, June felt Tom's breath against her cheek and she put her lips to his. They sat down after the song had finished, exhausted, it was already ten o'clock so he would be going in two hours.

"Shall we go upstairs Tom?"

"Yes, my darling." And he took her hand. Together they went up the stairs to share themselves with each other. Afterwards, June lay with her head on his chest.

"Fran still works at the charity shop during the week, yes?" Tom asked.

"Yes, yes she does. Why?"

"I was thinking - let's go out tomorrow, Beanie. We could go to the beach for the day, I can take the car."

"That's a bit risky, Tom," she frowned.

"No, look, if we wait for Fran to leave, it only leaves Mike at home and he'll be putting the TV on as soon as she goes, we know he does that."

June smiled, "True."

"The other two houses are quite a distance away and they're both young couples that work so we know it's like a ghost town during the week." They had bought their house because it was quite isolated, they had a farm and a meadow opposite and there were just four houses in the immediate area: June and Tom's and Fran and Mike's, but with an amount of land separating the two, then there were two semis, which were even further away. June gave it some thought and agreed that it would be possible to get out of the house after nine o'clock.

"We'd have to be back by four though Tom, Fran's back not long after that.

"Yes, that's no problem. If we drive, we can be at the coast in about an hour and home by three." June was excited at the prospect of going out with her husband, she would be ready for 9 am.

"Just as well I bought the dresses. I'll wear the other one tomorrow."

"We'll have a good day Beanie, just like old times."

"Yes, it will be." June felt a wave of happiness that they had what felt like a date tomorrow.

They lay together, June drinking in the smell of her husband. At eleven-thirty he got up and dressed and laid back on the bed, patting his chest for her to put her head back down. They lay like that, he stroked her shoulders, she closed her eyes and the next thing she knew, her head was on the pillow. She closed her eyes to sleep, knowing she was alone.

CHAPTER 3

June awoke and looked at the clock: it was seven, giving her plenty of time to get ready. The weather was due to be another late summer scorcher that Septembers seemed to bring these days. She got up and showered, then went downstairs to have some breakfast. She went back upstairs to put a few items in a beach bag: sun cream, wipes and lipstick.

It had been forever since she had been to the beach as a young woman. She didn't have a clue what to take but decided that anything missing, they could buy while they were there. She took the dress she had not worn off its hanger and took a white cardigan out of a drawer - cardigans were one of the few items of clothing that were ageless. She put on a cotton bathrobe and watched from the window as Fran left for work, then went downstairs. She put their song on and closed her eyes. Why she always had to do this, she didn't know, but Mr James had said to do it and wait for Tom's voice, so she didn't want to deviate from what she had been told.

"Hello, Beanie," came the usual greeting that made June's stomach flip. She opened her eyes and saw Tom.

"Ready for our day out then?" he asked, smiling.

She kissed him and hurriedly took off her bathrobe and put the clothes on she had brought downstairs.

"Yep, all ready," she said as she picked up the bag. "Fran left a little while ago so let's go."

"You look lovely, by the way," he said as he kissed her again.

They walked outside to the garage, which was set back from the house, and Tom lifted the door. June handed him the keys and they got into the car, stopping to put the garage door back down. They were onto the road and on their way to their first outing of this special time together. It took just over an hour to get to the coast. Tom found somewhere to park, and they got out. As Tom was getting the parking ticket, a group of lads walked by June, who was waiting by the car. They stared at her and she wondered why they were looking; did they know her? One of them said "Hello gorgeous!" She was bemused and surprised, She'd forgotten what it felt like to have this happen and was flattered by the attention, not something she would have been when she was young, but for it to happen after so many years made her feel good. She was ashamed to say she enjoyed the compliment. She smiled back at the same moment as Tom came back, the lads looked forward and carried on walking when they saw she was with someone.

"Oy Beanie," he said with a smile, "I'm going to have to watch you, aren't I?"

She laughed "Yes I think you are, Tom. I forgot what it felt like to be so in demand," after the latter years of invisibility that she somehow felt she had had.

"Shall we walk down to the beach?" he asked.

"Yes, it looks lovely and it's really empty."

Even though it was September and not yet fully warm, it was warm enough to walk down and sit on the beach, which was empty, owing to it being a Monday, when most people were at work. June unrolled a towel that she'd brought, and they both sat on it and watched the sea gently lap in and out, Tom sat with June in front of him, her head against his shoulder and he kissed her hair.

"This is lovely, June, who'd have thought we'd be doing this now, today?"

"I know."

They sat in silence for a while, their hands intertwined, just enjoying being with each other. Suddenly, Tom jumped up. "Last one to paddle is a frog face!" and he ran down to the edge of the water, where he stood ankle-deep. June followed and stood next to him. "We need to do this again when we've bought something to swim in," said Tom.

"Are you mad? It's freezing!" she said.

They walked along the edge of the sea for what seemed like miles, they both kept looking back to marvel at how far they had come. They arrived at a little beachfront stall that sold ice-creams.

"Want one?" asked Tom.

"Yes please," she replied.

They approached the man running the stall and ordered two ice-cream cones. He handed June's to her with a smile and a cheeky wink - she really was not used to this but was finding it fun. They sat on the sea wall and ate their ice-creams.

"Do you remember when we were last here alone, Tom?"

"Erm, let me try and work it out. We'd been married six months or so, I think. We had fish and chips at that little place that's probably not even here now. You got your dress wet because you got hit by a big wave and got really annoyed with me because of the wave."

"No Tom, because you were *laughing*," she said, slapping his arm.

"Do you know, Beanie; I don't remember a single day where we didn't enjoy ourselves. I'm sure there were some but all I remember when I think back is a wonderful life."

"Me too," she said.

"Hey," he said, looking at something behind him. "There's a funfair. Shall we?"

"Oh, I don't know, Tom, I never liked those things at the best of times."

"Oh, go on love, let's just do a couple of rides, easy ones."

"OK, come on," she reluctantly agreed.

They walked over to the fair, where there was a kiosk to buy tokens. They just bought a few and found a ride that was not too extreme. They got on, and as it started, June questioned her judgement on agreeing to this, but the ride was fun, scary enough but not too bad. Then Tom pointed to the whip.

"Yes?" he asked.

She remembered it had always been one of his favourites at the fair, they walked over to it and stood watching. "Come on Beanie, just this once?"

The man running the rides saw June's

hesitation, but saw her boyfriend wanted to have a go, so walked over to them and said, "Come on darlin', you're only young once."

June and Tom exchanged a look and June replied, "I wouldn't count on that." The man smiled bemusedly but with that they both got into a car and were thrown about for quite a long time, as the rides always seemed a little longer when the fairgrounds were quiet. The man spun the car a few times, much to June's annoyance, but she knew Tom would be having the time of his life. When the ride finished, they got off, laughing and said goodbye to the man who had spun the car with such gusto.

"One more thing to see," said Tom. "We've got a couple of tokens left, let's do the Hall of Mirrors, we always used to love that."

June could not help thinking how easily pleased their generation were, no internet, or gaming, or streaming, whatever that was but she hears her children talk about it, they gave their last two tokens and entered the hall. The first mirror made them short and very wide.

"Do you still love me like that, Tom?" June laughed.

"No," he said, and she playfully slapped his arm. Tom grabbed her and kissed her, slowly moving her backwards to the wall, he lifted her dress and said, "Shall we Beanie?"

"I don't think so Mister," she replied although she found herself feeling excited.

"Can't blame a boy for trying," he said playfully.

"No, but that will," she said, pointing to a camera in the corner.

"Oops," he said. They didn't have CCTV in these things years ago.

It must have proved popular viewing, as the woman running the entry booth said, "Hope you enjoyed yourselves," in an exaggerated way.

"That was fun, wasn't it?" Tom asked.

"Yes, we haven't done that for years."

"Right, time we grabbed something to eat, as we've only got a couple of hours before we should head home."

They found a seafront restaurant that had their menu displayed outside: it all looked delicious. There were one or two people in there and they found a table by the window, where they could watch the world go by. The food did not disappoint: they both opted for fish and chips and sat talking until it was time to do the mammoth beach walk back to the car. They drove home silently and satisfied in their enjoyment at such a beautiful day.

They were home by three thirty, so plenty of time to put the car back in the garage and get out unseen. Fran usually got home about ten past four. The first thing June did when they got through the door was put the kettle on.

Tom came up to her and said, "You know that Hall of Mirrors thing that we tried?"

"No Tom, that *you* tried," she laughed.

The tea never got made, they went upstairs, showered together and made passionate love.

They spent the rest of the time in the conservatory, talking about old times. It seemed to them that they could never talk enough even though they had been together for over fifty years, so there was always something to recount about their time together. Friends, family, jobs, houses - they had shared so much of each other's lives, it's like they were one. As nine o'clock approached and they sat with a glass of wine together in the autumn darkness with just a candle to light them, June started to get that same feeling of dread at losing all of this even though it was only for a while.

"Tom?"

"Yes, darling?"

"I need to go shopping tomorrow. Shall we go out again together like we did today, it seemed to work out alright and we can have lunch somewhere?"

"Yes. We'll go out of town though, somewhere new. I don't think we should tempt too much fate by going to the usual supermarket. So, I'll see you at nine again tomorrow."

"OK, darling" June said, stroking his face

"I'll miss you."

"Not long to wait, my angel," he said and with that, he was gone.

June struggled to get from the plush cushion of her conservatory furniture, her bones giving off a little crack. She knew she was back and was amused by the difference she felt, she picked up the wine glasses, blew out the candle and went to bed, her dreams full of Tom.

June had been up for about an hour and had showered. She got the dress out that she would wear for their lunch date and went downstairs to have some breakfast. She was thinking of where they might go today, lost in thoughts of small country inns where they could have a meal and afterwards, walk in the country and enjoy the lovely weather. She started to think about the realities of how this strange situation could possibly be real, but she was living it. Like Mr James said, she was very lucky. Her doorbell rang. She thought it was probably the postman and got up to answer it. When she opened the door, her granddaughter Samantha was there and brushed past June, stomping into the kitchen.

"Samantha, whatever's wrong?" she asked.

"It's Mum," she replied. "I really can't take anymore of her moaning at me. 'Samantha do this, Samantha do that'… she's getting so stressed because Chris is going away and because I have a free this morning, she's asked me to do so many jobs. He never does anything, just lies around all day being waited on."

"Oh dear, sweetheart, did you have a row with your Mum then?"

"Yes," she said, tears beginning to well up. "We always seem to argue these days and I just can't take anymore. Can I stay here with you today, Nan?"

June was taken aback by this and really did not know what to say. "Well, I was thinking of going shopping," was all that came to mind.

"That's OK Nan, I can come or wait here, it's

up to you."

June did not know what to say next. If she turned her granddaughter away, she would feel mean but if she had her here, she would not be able to see Tom and she found that hard to bear. June decided to talk to Samantha and try to iron things out, but as soon as she started to reason, Samantha just cut her off and said "I'm not going home, Nan, I don't care what you say. I won't be any trouble - do you not want me here?"

"Oh darling, of course I do. Let me phone your Mum just to let her know you're with me today." Resigning herself to not seeing Tom until later, when Samantha had gone home. She rang Meghan.

"Hello Meg, just to let you know Sam's with me, apparently you had a bit of a falling out?"

"Yes Mum, she just flies off the handle at me so much these days. I think she thinks Chris is getting all the attention, which he's not. It's just getting him to do anything for himself is a chore, so I end up doing it then I ask Sam to help with a few chores now and then and this is what happens." Meghan sounded very stressed, which made June sympathetic to her daughter.

"Well, don't worry about Sam, I'll keep her here today, give the both of you some time out. Shall I send her back for tea?" June asked, trying to get an idea of when she could see Tom.

"Up to you, Mum, you can feed her if she wants to stay. I'll leave it to you."

"OK, sweetheart, I'll see what she says later. You try not to stress too much Meg; I know it's difficult. I'll spoil her today, might take her shopping for a bit of a treat."

"She'd love that, Mum. See you later."

June put the phone down, resigned not to see Tom for a while. He would understand, he always knew how hard Meg worked with the children and a job, he would be happy that June had been there to help out today, but that didn't stop her from being selfish and feeling disappointed she wouldn't see him as planned. She went back into the kitchen, where Samantha was helping herself to a biscuit.

"Sorry, Nan, didn't have breakfast before I stormed out."

"Come here," June said to her granddaughter and held out her arms. Samantha loved a Nanny cuddle; her Nan made the world a better place for her.

"Now," said June, "I thought we'd have a bit of girlie shopping time today, what do you say?"

Samantha's face lit up. "Yes please, Nan, we can window shop until we drop."

"Not only window shop sweetheart, but I also think we'll buy you something nice to wear to cheer you up. What do you say?"

"Oh Nanna, I do love you, you're always so kind." June did not feel totally kind as she hugged Samantha, thinking that it is an awful thing to feel so torn, but that she'd rather be with Tom.

"I'm just going to the loo, Nan," and she

sprang up the stairs, her mood lifted by the thought of a day with her Nan. When she came back down, she was holding a hanger over her finger with one of June's new dresses on it.

"Nan, this is lovely, erm... is it yours?" June looked stunned by the fact that she had left the dress hanging outside her wardrobe for Samantha to see on her way out of the bathroom.

"Do you like it?" she asked, playing for time.

"Yes, it's gorgeous."

"Well, good, good."

"You bought it for me, didn't you, Nan?" Samantha asked, giving June an excellent out from an awkward situation.

"Yes, yes, I bought it for you, as a surprise, do you like it?"

"I love it Nan, thank you so much," and she gave June a tight cuddle of excitement.

June smiled at losing one of her dresses so soon but thought it was far better than explaining that "*your grandad comes to me* every day for twelve hours and he's twenty-three and I'm twenty and I needed something to wear because I'm young again." *No, I'll just give her the dress*, thought June, that is far easier and will stop her children getting her committed.

June went upstairs and got dressed into her usual clothes, thinking of Tom all the time. She wondered if he knew he was coming at nine, if he had any concept of time where he was, he says he knows nothing of where he goes and she hoped he also had no idea of time, because she hated to think of him stuck somewhere not knowing what was happening. June often wondered where Tom went. If he had the answers to where it was, then she would know so much about the afterlife but sadly, he said there was no conscious memory of it. June brushed her hair and gave a quick check in the mirror, she looked neat and tidy. She checked her watch: it was nine-thirty, she should have had a girl looking back at her in the mirror by now, but today she was Nan.

Tom always said "family first", he would want her to be there for their children and grandchildren. She went downstairs and put her arm round Sam's shoulder.

"Come on sweetie, let's hit the High Street." Sam put her hand up to high-five and June readily obliged.

When they got there, they went in all manner of shops. June bought some scented candles.

"Do you need those, Nan?" asked Samantha, laughing.

"No, I just *want* them," said June in reply, knowing this would make her granddaughter laugh. They had always shared a humour, right from when Samantha was a young child and shared a love of music and dancing, which they often did when June babysat. Samantha had grown up with a close bond to June, which is why she chose June to come to whenever there was a problem between her and her mother; June was always a welcoming pair of arms for Samantha to come to in times of angst. Over her teenage years it had usually been boy trouble for Samantha but now and again it was the clash between her mother and herself, which June recognised at an early stage of Samantha's teenage years.

"So, shall we eat out, Samantha?" June knew this would be make her granddaughter feel that she was being made a fuss of and would hopefully ensure she went home happy.

"Oh yes please Nan, we can go to that new little Italian the other end of the High Street."

"Before that, is there any shop you'd like to go in for Nan to treat you?" June asked.

"Yes" replied Sam. "Can we go to that clothes shop opposite the chemist?"

"Yes, of course" said June, realising that was the one she had been in herself to get the dresses. They went in and Sam looked at almost everything in the shop, she held three items. "Can I try these on, Nan?"

"Of course, sweetie," and Sam disappeared into the fitting room. She tried each item on, one was a dress, the other two were stylish tops, all of them looked lovely on her. She emerged from the fitting room saying, "I'll have the dress thanks, Nan."

"Did you like them all, Samantha?" June asked.

"Yes" she answered.

"Then you'll have all three."

"No Nan, that's too generous."

June took all the items from Sam and walked to the till, Sam following. When she got there, she recognised the assistant from a few days ago. The assistant looked at June, then at Sam, who said, "Oh thanks so much Nan."

The assistant looked at June and said "Oh hi! Did your granddaughter like the clothes?"

"Oh, the dress?" replied Sam, "Yes, I did thanks, it was lovely."

"And what about the underwear, did it fit?"

Sam looked bemused and looked at June. "Did you get me underwear too, Nan?"

"Y-yes" answered June. "It's at home. Anyway, shall we pay for these bits?"

They paid and left the shop, June hoping

that Sam forgot about the conversation with the assistant, as she had no idea how to explain why the underwear had no labels on and has been washed. June began to get over her embarrassment and said, "Shall we go for something to eat now Sam?"

"Yes. Let's hit the Italian restaurant."

"Sounds good to me, sweetheart." June linked her arm through Sam's and they headed off for the restaurant. As Sam was ordering, June looked at her watch: it was four-thirty. She figured that if she was home by six and Sam left soon after, she was free to spend the evening with Tom. All is not lost - they can go out tomorrow but this evening they could watch a film and sit in the conservatory cuddled up watching the stars, weather permitting.

June and Sam ate a delicious meal of carbonara, washed down with ice cold lemon cordial. June bought Sam a delicious Italian ice cream dessert and at the end of the meal Sam said, "Oh Nan, thanks so much for that, it was delicious."

June felt a stab of pride that she had made her granddaughter's day fun after the sad start she had had to it. "Now sweet, are you ready to go home and see Mum? She does love you, you know."

"Yes, OK Nan, I will. I'll come back to yours and walk home from there."

June was relieved that Sam was happy to go home because had she not been, of course June would have let her stay, as her and Tom's loyalty was to their family first, but to miss an evening when they only had a limited number would be awful. They walked home and when they got to June's house Sam said she would do the half-hour walk home from there.

"Are you sure Samantha? You can come in, sweetheart."

"No, that's OK, Nan."

"Are you and your Mum going to be alright now?"

"Yes, I've had such a lovely day. I'll make up with Mum when I get home."

June felt a stab of relief. She hated family falling out because it always upset her, so she was happy that she could see Tom this evening and peace had been resumed between her daughter and granddaughter. Sam gave her Nan a kiss and hugged her.

"I do love you, Nan. Thanks for a brilliant day and for my clothes."

"You're more than welcome, sweetheart, we'll do it again soon," and she watched Sam walk down the road holding her gifts.

June looked at her watch: it was six-fifteen. She went inside and didn't bother to do anything other than throw her bag down and go into the lounge to put the record on. As she heard it start, she closed her eyes and felt the excitement and anticipation that these visits brought then she heard his voice.

"Hello Beanie," and she opened her eyes to see her Tom, she ran to him and threw herself into his arms.

"Oh Tom, I'm so very sorry it's so late." She told him about Samantha, the argument with her mother and how she sacrificed her own day out to take Samantha shopping.

"That's absolutely fine, Beanie. Our children come first," and she looked at this twenty-three-year-old man talking about his children who were years older than him. Yet again, this experience blew her mind.

"We can have a nice evening, Beanie, and go out tomorrow."

"Yes, we will. Did you know it was later than we planned when you weren't here?"

"I told you Beanie, I really don't remember anything that happens when I'm not with you. I'm not even sure where I go."

"If you knew, it would probably answer a lot of questions about what happens to us," she said.

"Yes, but maybe that's why I don't remember it, I have no recollection of what happens between visits." He took her face in his hands. "Anyway, I'm here now so let's just enjoy each other."

"We will," she replied, "But I've been out

most of the day and feel grimy so I'll just have a shower."

"No, you won't" he said. June looked at him quizzically as he smiled and said, "*We'll* have a shower."

She laughed and immediately felt excited at getting into the water naked with him, then they would make love. They got under the hot shower, he immediately began to explore her body, he soaped her and when he'd finished washing her, he turned her round and put his hands on her breasts, putting himself inside her. She moaned with excitement and pushed herself against him as they both felt the pleasure only the two of them could feel together. Afterwards, they went downstairs and had tea. They put the TV on and saw that the remake of "War of the Worlds" was on. They'd both enjoyed the original and thought they'd give the remake a go, surprisingly enjoying it and daring to say they found it better than the original. They cuddled as they watched TV. June enjoyed their physical closeness. She was still not used to her young reflection whenever she looked in the mirror; it still felt very strange to see a young June looking back at her. After the film, they went into the conservatory, June made them both tea and they sat talking about the children. Tom said he wondered if Jane would ever marry because she had such a good career in London. They knew she had a boyfriend who she met recently but she was always quite private about her life, even with her parents, so they really couldn't gauge whether she even wanted marriage and children.

"Do you miss them, Tom?" June asked.

"Do you know what June, it's really strange but it's almost like I've gone through some sort of transition, I can't explain it very well, but although I still care for them deeply, I don't feel I should be with them. It's almost like dying removes the need to be with those we love but we still care. I don't expect that to make sense, it doesn't even make sense to me and I'm the one feeling it."

"That's interesting," June replied, "And good really, because otherwise our time together could be so much more difficult if you missed the children."

"Yes, I agree but that makes it sound like I don't care, but I care as much about them as before I died. I just know somehow I'm not meant to be with them anymore."

June was fascinated by this but glad for Tom as, if he missed them, coming back would be a painful experience for him. Just then, the external light in the garden came on and they looked out to see a fox, both of them found it to be a beautiful creature. It momentarily looked at them and then was gone.

"That was a quick visit," June said, reminding her of how quickly Tom disappeared. She stifled a yawn; it was midnight already.

"Oh Beanie, you're tired, darling."

"Yes, a day shopping with Samantha has worn me out but I don't want to go to bed yet Tom, I'll miss you if I sleep."

"Who said anything about sleep, Beanie?" said Tom, winking.

She laughed, she adored making love to him and this man in his twenties was more than happy to accommodate those desires. They climbed the stairs and undressed in the bedroom. Getting into bed, he kissed her and put his hand between her legs to find her ready for him. He touched her and kissed her breasts, by the time he was inside her, she was writhing in pleasure. They made love and lay together, June fighting the urge to sleep. Her head lay on his shoulder, his arm around her, stroking her back. The next thing June knew, the sun was peeping through the curtains. She felt Tom's lips on hers.

"I love you, Beanie, I'll see you later darling," and she reached out to take him in her arms but felt nothing there, she opened her eyes, he was gone.

June was showered and in her gown ready to put the record on, with her clothes laid out next to her. She hoped there would be no interruptions today. As the song started to play, she closed her eyes and waited; she heard the now familiar voice.

"Hello Beanie." She turned to see Tom, they kissed. "Where shall we go today?" he asked, "Any ideas?"

"I thought we could go for a drive, Tom, and find a little country inn for lunch."

"Sounds wonderful," replied Tom.

June got dressed and they climbed into the car. Once on the open road they headed for a rural area they used to visit when they were young, properly young that is. They stopped at the edge of a forest and parked the car. As they walked into the forest holding hands and passing occasional people, they would smile and say, "Good morning."

After a while, they came to a log and sat down. June put her head on Tom's shoulder. "Tom?" she asked.

"Yes darling?"

"Do you ever wonder what will happen to

you after the two weeks, I mean where will you or your soul or whatever, where will it go for ever?"

"I suppose so but it's odd, Beanie, it's almost like I have no interest in anything other than the visits. I don't get it, but wherever it is I feel it will be nothing to fear. Thoughts are so different now. Before I questioned everything but it's almost like whatever this is, my mind has only need for existence in whatever form that existence takes. Like now, I am just satisfied to be. The difference I feel with you is an overwhelming feeling of love, that never changes, but to question why I'm here is not something I have a want to do. I'm hopeless at explaining it, Beanie but it's like a complete and utter inner peace."

"Wow Tom, that sounds rather lovely."

"Yes, it is. It's like what was meant to be will be, even leaving those I love, even leaving you after two weeks will break my heart, but it won't because it's meant to be that way, if that makes sense."

"Yes, kind of," June replied. "I know it'll break my heart not to see you again, but I feel privileged to have had what we've got right now, not many get this chance."

"Yes, we're very lucky. It's weird - but a lot of fun, eh?"

He kissed her just as an elderly couple were walking past, June and Tom laughed and said, "Sorry."

The couple looked at them sweetly and the woman said, "Oh no, don't be. We were like that once. Make the most of being young. It doesn't last, you know."

When they'd gone past, Tom looked at his watch and said, "About another seven hours to be precise." Then getting up, he said, "Come on, Beanie, let's finish this walk and then find that little inn you want."

He held out his hand and pulled her up to him, then arm in arm they walked for another half an hour before going back to the car. They drove for a few miles, passing a few pubs until they found one that they liked the look of. It had a thatched roof and a sign that said, "Good Food and a Warm Welcome".

They parked and went inside. It was empty, apart from three people at the bar. The barman smiled at Tom and June as they went to the bar.

"Are you serving food at the moment?" Tom asked.

"Yes sir, in the restaurant area. You're welcome to take a seat." He pointed toward a cosy dining area. Tom and June went over and saw there was one other couple, already eating their meal. They sat at a table by the window and a waitress came over with a menu, telling them the Chef's specials for that day. They chose from the menu and waited for the waitress to come back. Tom took June's hand across the table and stroked it, both sitting in silence just enjoying and appreciating the moment. After they had eaten and sat for a while longer, Tom looked at the clock in the restaurant.

"We'd better be heading home, Beanie,

before our Fran gets home from work." June was enjoying the tranquillity of their surroundings but reluctantly agreed; they paid the bill and left for the drive home. The journey home was uneventful, and they arrived in plenty of time to put the car away and go in unseen. Once in, they sat drinking tea and talking more about old times, a lot of "Do you remember when...?" sentences. As they sat talking, they were interrupted by the doorbell ringing. June looked startled and looked at Tom whispering, "Upstairs." They hurriedly went up the stairs and into the bedroom, where they heard the doorbell go again, shortly followed by a key being put into the lock, it was Meghan calling in to see her Mum on her way home from work. June's sense of panic was extreme. She prayed Meghan wouldn't come upstairs. She heard Meghan go into the kitchen and could hear cupboards being opened and crockery clanking, *what on earth could Meg want*, she wondered? Then finally the noise stopped and she heard the water tap being turned on, then a final bang before silence. June didn't have a clue what Meg was doing now. She heard nothing and with her heart in her mouth, wondered if she was coming up the stairs, maybe to check on her mother. She looked at Tom and surprisingly saw he was in a state of shock that looked even worse than hers. "Tom" she whispered, "Are you alright?"

"I think so, Beanie, I feel like I'm being told to go."

"What do you mean go? June asked.

"I can't stay here; I just know it." He looked at her. "It feels strange June, it's like there's a magnet pulling me away from you."

At that moment, they heard the rattle of Meghan's keys as she picked them up to leave. As she shut the door behind her, Tom looked relieved.

"Do you still feel it, Tom?"

"No, no, it's gone, whatever it was, it's over." He took June's hand. "I really thought I was going to be taken away from you, but I have no idea why. It must be something to do with Meghan."

"Yes, I remember Mr James saying that our children must never be allowed to see you, or your visits would stop but I have no idea why. I think I'll phone him tomorrow and see if he knows why. I'm curious."

June kissed Tom and said, "Don't worry, my darling, you're still here, we'll find out what that was all about, hopefully."

He looked at ease and they went downstairs together to see if they could find out what Meghan had been doing. The mystery of the noise was solved as June saw that her daughter had put a beautiful bouquet of flowers into a vase and next to this was a note that read, *"Hi Mum, just popped in the see if you were OK. I bought you these to cheer you up. See you Saturday at 11. Love you loads. Meg"*.

"Oh, look Tom," she said, "Aren't they lovely?" and she bent to smell them.

"Yes," he replied. "They are. She's a lovely

daughter isn't she, checking on you and being so thoughtful? We did good Beanie; we have great children."

They spent the rest of the time mainly sitting in the conservatory together, sometimes talking, sometimes just enough to sit silently and cuddle. When it began to get dark, they went through to the lounge to play music from their collection and dance together. Tom loved dancing with her and she loved being with her soulmate again, activities that may seem boring to many were so different for these two people who had been given a chance to enjoy each other again. With an hour to go, they went upstairs to make love and then lay together until her head slowly sank into the pillow as her husband disappeared. She would call Mr James in the morning to ask more about the phenomena of what had happened to Tom when Meghan had been in the house but meanwhile, she'd get up and watch some TV. As she came down the stairs the phone rang, she answered it, it was Meghan.

"Hello Mum," she said.

"Oh, Meg, sorry, I should have phoned you to say thanks for those beautiful flowers. That was so sweet."

"That's OK Mum. Did you have a good day? Where were you?"

"I went out walking again," June said, "I can get lost in my thoughts when I walk, it's awfully therapeutic you know."

"Yes, I imagine it is. As long as you're alright though and coping on your own?"

"Yes Meg, I'm absolutely fine. I have my moments but it's all part of the process. Anyway, how are you and Samantha?" she asked, wanting to change the subject to save her from having to lie to her daughter.

"We're fine Mum. She had a wonderful day with you, she was a different girl. We all get stressed at the moment and sometimes it just spills over. That's families, eh?" Meghan laughed.

"Indeed. You three had your disagreements as I remember and when your Dad caught Paul having a cigarette that day, it almost started world war three."

"Oh God yes, I'd forgotten about that. Wasn't he really sick afterwards though and it put him off for life?"

"Yes, he was and I remember Dad telling him it served him right."

"Anyway Mum, I'll leave you in peace now. Are you looking forward to Saturday?"

"Yes, very much, I can't wait."

They said their goodbyes and June felt a bit guilty that although she was looking forward to seeing her family it would make seeing Tom later than she would have liked. But it was just the way it was and she immediately reprimanded herself for being selfish.

That night, June went to bed excited as always for the next day.

CHAPTER 4

She awoke at seven, wondering what the day would bring. Being in sole control of times for Tom's visit was difficult. They never actually arranged or spoke about what they could do today, but an idea was formulating in her mind. The little pub they had stopped at yesterday offered accommodation and she wondered if there was any way her and Tom could spend a night away together. If he came to her at 5 pm, they could drive to the pub, book in and leave to come home at dawn. They could then park the car up the road and walk from there so as not to disturb anyone or be seen. Tom could come back at 9 am and go and get the car after Fran had left for work. It seemed like a perfect plan and a way they could get to spend somewhere overnight.

June got ready, had breakfast and phoned for a taxi to take her to the supermarket - she had never learnt to drive. It had never really interested her and Tom and she went most places together, apart from her keep fit, or sometimes she would go to the local shops alone, which she could walk to. However, now she was alone, she shopped so rarely that when she did have to get more than usual to stock up, so she just rang for a taxi. Today she would get her shopping and something nice to wear tonight because her supermarket had a great choice of clothing for all ages, thank goodness. She chose a short, black, classically styled dress and some heels. She hadn't worn heels for a long time and hoped that she would be able to walk in them. She also chose some matching underwear, black lace of course, and as she paid for her shopping, she was feeling even more excited about tonight. When she got home, she looked up the number of the pub and rang, asking if they had any rooms free. The man on the other end asked what she'd require and when she said a double, he immediately told her they had some available. He asked what time they would be arriving, she said six o'clock this evening and he said he was looking forward to seeing them. So, the deed was done, Tom would be so excited to know they were going to spend a night together away. They could have a lovely meal and a drink then go to their room for some romantic time - maybe take a bottle of champagne up with them. It didn't matter if they didn't sleep until after they left, June could sleep for a few hours when she got home before getting Tom back to pick up the car. She felt very proud of herself for planning something so different and her mind went back to yesterday and Meghan's visit, the effect it had on Tom and she picked up the phone again, getting Mr James's card out of a drawer and dialling his number.

He answered quickly, "Hello."

"Hello, Mr James, it's June Reader."

"Oh, hello Mrs Reader, how are you getting on? Did you take advantage of the extra time?" he asked.

"Yes, yes, I did and I can't thank you enough, it's been surreal and strange but we've had so much fun."

"Good, I'm glad. I imagine you have one or two questions."

"Yes, I do. Obviously, I'm intrigued as to how the whole thing works, I mean, where does Tom go? Where does he come from?"

"I can't give you any answers on that, I'm afraid, I don't even know myself. I am simply tasked with making it known to true soulmates that they can do this. There are more of you than you imagine out there, you might be standing next to a couple in a shop and you wouldn't know they are revisits like your own."

"How come Tom can't remember anything about it when he visits?"

"Again, June," replied Mr James, "I can't answer that."

"Who gives you the instructions of who to give these visits to?" asked June.

"I just can't share that with you, I'm sorry." June knew that it was pointless to ask any more, he was not going to give any more information, she decided to move on and ask him about Tom's reaction to Meghan.

"We had a close shave the other day" she said.

"Oh, why?" he enquired.

"Well, our daughter let herself in while Tom was here and we hid in the bedroom, but I was really surprised to see Tom quite so terrified and he said he felt strange. You said the children shouldn't see him, but Meg was downstairs, why would this affect him? It's just curiosity."

"Well," Mr James replied, "Where your husband comes from is not anywhere as we know it, they are souls that travel to a place to await their final destination. As I told you on my visit to you, the being that visits you - and the other people who have this experience - is made up of vibrations that can dissipate in a moment. To all intents and purposes, he is your husband but they cannot take on actual solid physical forms that are the same as you and me so these people are made up of vibrations that can provide a solid form for the time they are with you. You would find that if your children were in a situation where they are in close danger of seeing him, he would disappear, as would your physical appearance change back to what you really are. What happened to your husband the other day was that he was prematurely being pulled back, the danger of being seen was close but obviously not close enough to take him away. You would have found that if your daughter had approached the room you were in, then he would have gone. The feeling he would have had is a trauma to his vibrational self, this is caused by his will not wanting his children to undergo any shock or pain in seeing you both transformed as you are on the visits. It's like a protection thing for the family, but as the trauma is so dramatic, his vibrational self will be destroyed. I don't expect any of this to make sense though, I'm sorry."

"To be honest, Mr James, it makes no less sense than this whole experience, so I'll take that as an explanation even though I don't understand it. Thank you so much for running through it, at least I can tell Tom why he felt so awful."

"Well, no harm done but carry on being as careful as you obviously have been."

They said their goodbyes and June felt no more at ease about what had happened, because none of this entire thing made sense and her mind just couldn't absorb how weird it all was.

June looked at the clock and saw it was past lunchtime and knowing she had a lovely meal to look forward to later, decided to just have a cup of tea and a couple of biscuits then a quick lie-down before getting ready for tonight. She fell asleep and woke in time to shower and prepare for Tom's visit. She brought her new dress downstairs with the heels which she had tried on for size. At five o'clock she put the record on and stood with her eyes closed; she heard his voice.

"Hello, Beanie," and as ever, her heart skipped a beat.

They kissed, Tom looked at the clock and

said, "It's going to be a late one."

"Yes," she said as she got dressed, first putting on the black underwear to which Tom whistled and said, "Wow, gorgeous. Come here."

She laughed, "No, we've got a date," and she slipped on the short little dress she'd bought, then put the heels on.

"Well, how do I look?"

"You look beautiful, do we have to go out?" he winked at her.

"Yes, we're going to that pub again, the one we went to yesterday. We're going to have a meal and I've booked a room."

Tom looked puzzled. "How is that going to work?"

She explained the whole plan to him, about getting home early then him coming back at 9 am to get the car.

"Well, well Beanie, you've put a lot of thought into this."

"I certainly have. I just really loved that restaurant and thought wouldn't it be nice to have a romantic night away?"

"I'm all for that, but how are we going to get there without being seen by the neighbours?"

"It's Fran's French class on Thursdays: she goes straight from work and doesn't get home until after six."

"Perfect," said Tom and he gave June his arm as they left the house.

They drove for almost an hour and found the pub, it looked even better as the twilight of the September evening made the lights outside twinkle and sparkle. The beamed exterior looked as good as the inside.

They went in and June said to the barman, "We have a meal and a room booked in the name of Reader."

He called for somebody who came and took them through to the restaurant, which was a bit fuller today; they didn't get a choice of table but the one they were offered was in a quiet little alcove where they felt comfortable. The waiter brought them menus and asked if they would like drinks. They ordered a bottle of wine to have with their meal and some water. The waiter went and before they looked at the menu, Tom reached over and stroked June's face.

"You really are the most beautiful woman in the world, you know," he said lovingly.

She put her hand on his and said, "I love you Tom, I really do."

She felt a stab of desire so decided to look at the menu and concentrate on the food, after which they could go to their room and touch each other all night if they wished. They ate their meal unhurriedly and then sat in the bar for a while, having cocktails and talking about their close shave with Meghan. June told him all about her conversation with Mr James as best she could remember and Tom looked thoughtfully at her. What she was saying didn't really make sense but, like her, he thought this whole thing didn't make sense.

"So, I'm just a load of old vibrations, Beanie?"

"It appears so, darling."

"Well, let's go up to the room shall we and you can show this load of vibrations that underwear again."

They got up from the table and asked the barman for their room key. He handed them a key. "It's room 14," he said pleasantly. They asked if they could settle the bill now as they would be leaving very early.

"Yes of course," he replied and June gave him her bank card.

"When you go in the morning, there's a little reception area out there." He pointed to a hallway. "Just leave the key on the counter." They thanked him and said they would and wished him goodnight.

When they got to the room, they both fell on the bed.

"Ooh, comfy," said June.

Tom climbed on top of her and said, "I do love that dress, Beanie."

"Do you?"

"Yes, but you know how I think it could look better?"

"No," she said intrigued.

He pointed to a chair in the room - "If it was on that chair."

She got up and slowly took the dress off, revealing her beautiful figure in the black lace underwear. He pulled her to him as he sat on the bed and began to kiss her stomach gently. June found this erotic and she bent down to find his mouth with hers. She began to undo his shirt and slip it off. He undid her bra and she let it fall to the floor, pressing her breasts again his chest as they kissed passionately. June enjoyed their lovemaking at home but being here made it even more romantic and sexy. She stood up and took her panties off as Tom undressed. He laid her on the bed and climbed on top of her and they made love, both overwhelmed with the amount of desire they felt.

Afterwards, they lay together talking about what to do tomorrow and June talking about how much she missed him when he was not with her. They kissed and June felt that Tom was ready to make love again, which they did with as much passion as the first time. Afterwards, they lay together, determined that they would stay awake until 4 am, when they would silently leave and go home. June put her head on his chest as he stroked her hair.

June awoke to see the sun streaming through the curtains, she wondered where she was for a moment then turned to the clock by the bed, it was seven o'clock. She looked next to her in the bed and it was empty, leaving just an imprint in the pillow. They had clearly both overslept and Tom would have gone at 6 am.

She jumped up and looked in the mirror and saw that she was seventy-four again, stuck in a hotel room where a twenty-year-old had booked in the night before.

"Think! Think, June!" she said out loud to herself.

She had no idea what to do, the car was outside, she couldn't get home but the only place she could get Tom to come back was from their home. She sat on the edge of the bed and started to formulate a plan.

She phoned reception, a young woman answered "Hello, Reception."

"Oh, hello yes, this is room 14, we were going to check out today but I wondered, is it possible to book it for one more night?"

"Just one moment," said the woman and June heard the rustling of pages being turned while the woman checked, June didn't breathe until the woman's voice said "Yes, that's absolutely fine."

"Oh, thank you so much," said June.

"Would you both like breakfast, it's being served until ten?"

"No thank you," said June, "We'll be going out soon, we'll come back later."

"That's fine Madam, we'll see you later. Will you require a reservation for the restaurant tonight?"

"No, I don't think so. Thank you though."

So, that was phase one of the plan put together. She now just had to get home and get

Tom, so that they could return for the car. They would make their excuses later about not being able to stay tonight, but it meant that the car could be left for a while without arousing suspicion, which, had she just left and gone home after they had only booked for one night, their car left in the car park would have done. Now she only had to get home. She could book a taxi but didn't have the number of any taxi service in this area. She rang Reception again. The woman answered.

"Oh hello, do you have a local taxi firm's number?"

"Yes, of course Madam, just one moment. OK, here it is," and she gave June the number.

June thanked her again and decided to get dressed immediately and, *this is the tricky bit*, she thought, get down the stairs and out of the door without being seen. She put the black dress back on, which was snug to say the least, and then the heels, which were not as easy to walk in as when she was wearing them last night. Fortunately, she had brought a big coat with her, which she could put on over the top of the dress which did look rather ridiculous on her now aged figure, as it was far too tight and noticeably short.

She slipped the room key in her bag and rang for a taxi. They said it would be about fifteen minutes and June asked that she be picked up at the front of the pub, where she could wait out of sight of the building. She was silently reprimanding herself and Tom for oversleeping, as she still had the most stressful part to go yet - getting out unseen. She left the room and walked silently along the carpeted corridor, getting to the top of the stairs and heard voices below in the Reception area. It was the woman she had spoken to on the phone and a man's voice: they were discussing menus and bookings for the evening restaurant service. June was trapped at the top of the stairs, hoping neither of them came up. She began to despair and wanted to cry, not knowing what on earth to do in this situation. If she went downstairs and they saw her, being such a small hotel, they would know exactly what guests they had. She also began to worry that the taxi would arrive and would come into Reception to ask who had booked it, June was getting frantic.

Suddenly, she heard the man say, "Do you want to make sure everyone's OK in the breakfast room? I've got to make a phone call in the office."

June breathed a sigh of relief as she heard the door open and the woman go through it, then the man's voice in the distance speaking on the phone. She hurried down the stairs, getting to the door and running across the gravelled car park in heels that she could hardly walk in. She thought she must have looked a sight but finally got to the front of the car park and stood slightly to the right of the pub, where trees and bushes would hide her from view. She waited about four minutes when she saw the taxi arrive and she stuck out her arm, climbing in with her coat buttoned up to the neck.

Once in, she collapsed back on the seat with another sigh of relief and felt quite proud of successfully pulling off her escape. The cab pulled up at the bottom of her drive. She got out and rushed inside, relieved to shut her front door. She decided to shower and have some breakfast, knowing that as the room was booked for tonight, there was no need to hurry back for the car.

Poor Tom. She wondered if he was frantic about oversleeping and leaving her, or whether he even knew he had?

It was 10 am when she put their song on and she closed her eyes.

"Hello Beanie," said the familiar voice.

She opened her eyes to see her beloved husband. "Hello darling," and was just about to recount what happened but he said, "Oh God, darling, are you alright? I'm so sorry I left you. We fell asleep, didn't we?"

She realised he remembered everything that happened when he was here with her. "Yes, Tom. It was awful," and she recounted her whole escape operation to him.

"So, we've got to go back?" he said.

"Yes, the car's there. Give me a couple of minutes and I'll get dressed and phone for a taxi." She phoned a different taxi company than the one she usually used and it came about ten minutes later. They both got in and headed for the inn. When they got there, they entered via Reception, to be greeted by the woman June had spoken to on the phone.

"Hello," she smiled at them both.

"Hello," replied June. "We've just popped back for something." The woman said she hoped they had a nice day and June and Tom climbed the stairs to their room.

Tom said, "Why don't we go out somewhere, come back here for a meal later and tell the barman we've decided not to stay overnight after all, but we'll still pay for the room? Then we can go home afterwards, leave the car in the next road and walk home. It'll only be about nine o'clock but it's dark by then; we can sneak in and the neighbours won't see us."

"Alright, Tom, that sounds good. Shall we find that forest again - it's not too far away from here?"

"Yes, we'll reserve a table for six o'clock on our way out."

"Come on then," said June, as she went to open the door.

"Not so fast," Tom said, as he took her hand. "We might as well make the most of the room if we're not having it overnight. They kissed and both went towards the bed.

They found the forest and the parking area and got out of the car. They stood there for a few moments, admiring the beauty of the sunlight falling between the trees. Both of them had always found forests to be magical places and especially right now... there was something extra special about where they were, being young, with the one you love and walking hand in hand through such a beautiful place. As they emerged from the trees they came to a large open field, there were a few other people dotted around. It was another one of those late summer days that happened in September and people were enjoying the sun in the knowledge that soon the oppression of winter would be here to force them indoors, with their heating on and long nights of darkness.

June lay her coat on the grass and they both sat down, watching two young boys playing football. The woman they were with offered them bottles of water, which the boys took and gulped down thirstily, gave back and carried on playing football. There was an old couple on a bench, occasionally speaking but looking ahead and enjoying the air.

"Look at them Tom, that's us."

"Kind of," he said. "It *was* us before..." He never wanted to say the words "before/when I died", he said it made him uncomfortable to say those words, which was odd for someone who was not a physical being to feel discomfort at saying things, but then June remembered Mr James talking about the vibrations that he was made up of and she thought maybe saying something that caused those he loved such pain made him feel sad.

"I wonder if they'll get any extra time, Tom?"

"Well, that depends on whether they are true soulmates," he replied.

"Yes, that was the reason we have been put together for this extra time. Mr James said that when we look around, we may not even know that we are in the presence of others that are in the same situation as us, that fascinates me. All those young couples we see, who knows?"

"Yes, they could be the same as us. I don't really fancy asking anyone though, do you? Can you imagine? We'd get carted off!" Tom laughed.

June giggled and swung round to lay her head on Tom's lap. He stroked her hair. She would really miss this closeness when he went but most of all, she would just miss his presence. "Looking forward to the barbecue tomorrow?" he asked her.

"Yes, very much so. It'll be nice to have the kids all in one place. I haven't seen them all together since the...the other day." She was reluctant to say the word funeral. "I haven't even spoken to Jane but she's always so busy. I'm very proud of her -she really stuck at it to become a lawyer. Goodness knows where she got her brains."

"Hey, do you mind?" said Tom "Me, obviously."

The boys had stopped playing football and were sitting down to a picnic that the woman had carefully laid out for them. They were hungry, as June thought boys always were. She remembered Paul eating them out of house and home, unlike the girls who would have their little bits and pieces like cheese and crackers. Paul would open the fridge and demolish whatever he could, much to her annoyance sometimes, especially when it was the last of the cheese or milk, and he never thought to let her know.

The elderly couple got up off the bench and began to walk along the path. June watched them intently, thinking how invisible they would be to the young. This was something that never ceased to surprise her now, in her present form. She felt she got more attention as a young woman, particularly from men who would want to be charming and smile at her a lot; other young people also noticed them. It was almost like they had a light that shone brightly as a young couple, but that light dimmed when she was back in her older form and most people seemed to look through her. Sometimes she wanted to scream that she was young once. June was vain enough to acknowledge that she missed attention as she got older, she missed the benefits of youth - not only physically, but missed her presence being so bold and bright as it is now.

Tom laid back on the grass, staring up at the sky. "I wonder if my other home is up there, Beanie?"

She looked up at the clouds floating gently

by. "Maybe. It's a shame you can't remember where you go - it'd be so interesting."

"I know darling, I know."

June sat up and kissed Tom; a long kiss that young couples could do in public. He responded by saying, "I love you so much, I really do."

"I'm hungry, Tom." She looked around in the distance. "Look, there's a little café over there... shall we walk over to it?" The café was on the far side of the field.

"Yes, come on, sounds like a good idea." He jumped up and put his hand out to pull her. They walked slowly arm in arm across the field, saying hello to the woman and the two boys as they passed them. They got to the café. The menu wasn't very big but they decided on two portions of chips and a soft drink; they would be eating at the pub later so didn't want to have too much to eat. The food at the pub was amazing and they would probably have two or three courses. Chips now would do just fine.

They sat outside the café then walked back toward the forest after they'd finished. They got halfway across the field when the sky opened and they found themselves getting drenched. June put her coat on and they started to run, getting to the edge of the forest soaking wet. The forest stayed relatively dry with occasional slippery patches where the trees were parted. At one of these wet patches June slipped over and immediately felt a pain in her ankle so intense it made her cry.

"June!" Tom tried to pull her up but her ankle hurt too much.

"Ow! Tom, I don't know what I've done."

"Just give it a minute and we'll see if you can walk."

They waited for a minute then Tom helped June get up. She couldn't put any weight on the ankle and it was swelling up as he watched. He ended up carrying her back to the car and putting her in the front seat, her ankle was swollen and blue.

"We're going to need to get you to a

hospital."

"We can't, Tom, we'll have to deal with it."

"Why? We can go to A&E, there's one in town. It doesn't matter if we don't get our meal later, we can go next week. The main thing now is to get that ankle looked at, it's only one o'clock, we've got until five to get home before Fran. We can't really go for the meal tonight; you won't be able to walk from the car if we park it a distance away and we can't drive the car all the way home and risk being seen." Tom pulled away and headed for the hospital. When they got there June could hobble on her ankle and they both went up to Reception where they waited to speak to someone. A man on the desk said, "Hello, how we can help?"

"My wife fell over and has done something to her ankle, I don't think it's broken but could someone look at it?"

"Of course," said the man. "Your name?" and he started to type into a computer.

"June Reader" replied June, the man began to type it in then said, "Date of birth?"

June's eyes opened wide at the question "Erm..." The man looked up at her; she stared back. "Sorry my lovely," he said, "What is your date of birth?"

June remained silent; the man looked at Tom, puzzled.

"What is your wife's date of birth?" he asked again.

June turned to Tom and said, "Do you know what, darling, this ankle is feeling better by the second. Can I leave it? I really don't think I need to take up your time."

"Well," said the man, "Now you're here I really think it would be best for someone to take a quick look."

"No, really," said June, "I'll just go to my GP when I get home. I'll get an evening appointment as an emergency."

"Are you sure?" said the kind man at the desk.

"Yes, yes. Come on Tom, it feels virtually better."

Tom tried to support June as best he could

while she attempted to walk confidently out of the hospital with an ankle that was extreme agony.

Once outside she bent over and let out a large "*O u c h!*" then said, "There's no way I could have given my date of birth. We're going to have to go back to the hotel and soak it in cold water, Tom. I think it's sprained."

"OK, let's get you back there and Doctor Tom will make you better. We'll stop at a pharmacy and get some bandage to support it. My poor little Beanie, you are a brave girl."

"Actually, it really doesn't feel half as bad as it did when it happened. If it's better later, can we still stay for the meal?"

"But what about the walk from the car tonight when we get back?"

"We'll just park the car a bit nearer than we'd planned and you can carry me. Oh, please Tom, I really want to keep our date."

"We'll see," he said, kissing her head.

When they got back to the hotel June was limping. They managed to get up to their room with Tom helping her up the stairs. They got in the room and Tom ran a cold bath where June put her foot in and soaked it. It immediately felt a lot better, after a while he took it out, dried it and put the ankle support on her that the pharmacist had given them. She limped around the room, Tom told her to lay on the bed and rest it, he rang Reception and asked for some tea to be brought to the room, they drank their tea laughing about the look on June's face when the man at the hospital had asked for her date of birth.

They lay on the bed until it was time to go down to the bar, they had packed the few things they had brought and neatened the room.

They were greeted by the friendly barman, who saw June limping in with a bandage round her ankle. Fortunately, she had left the heels at home this morning and worn her flats.

"What happened to you?" he asked

"We went for a walk," June replied, "and stupid me slipped over."

"Did you go to the hospital?" asked the barman, concerned.

"No, it's only a sprain. A bit of support and it'll be better in no time," she said, not feeling even slightly convinced herself by her answer as she felt her ankle throbbing.

"Oh well, if you're sure. What can I get you?" he asked and they ordered a bottle of red, booking a table for a meal at the same time. "I wonder if my ankle will still be swollen when you've gone, Tom?" June said after they had sat down.

"I don't know, possibly" he said.

"Oh dear, what am I going to tell the children tomorrow?"

"Exactly what happened Beanie, you were out walking and slipped."

"Yes, I suppose so. They'll make a big fuss about me doing too much," June said with a sigh.

"Well, that's because they worry about you, now you're on your own. Just tell them you had the wrong shoes on to walk in or something and won't be doing that again... something to put their minds at ease."

"Good thinking, Tom. You always were the clever one of the partnership," she laughed.

The waitress came over to take them to their table, which she did slowly, seeing June's limp. They were seated at the table they first sat at when they found this little place, somehow that was meaningful to them, it had led to them spending a night out together even though it didn't quite go according to plan. They ordered three courses and afterwards, sat drinking a coffee, musing at their experience so far and discussing plans when they got home.

Fran would be watching TV by the time they got back, her lounge was at the rear of the house, her dining room at the front so they were relatively safe. They didn't want to take the car all the way back to the house though, as they felt the noise of a car pulling up on the drive of their house that late may cause Fran to check if she hears, she has always been a good neighbour to them. She means no harm or interference in her watchfulness but being remote, the two households tended to look out for each other over the years. Now June was on her own too, Fran felt even more vigilant about looking out for her.

They left the restaurant at eight o'clock, giving them plenty of time for the drive home and to walk from the car at the other end.

When they were nearly there, June said, "Tom, park at the beginning of our road where there are more houses, we don't know anyone there and there's always quite a few cars parked along it, we'll just blend in.

"Yes OK," said Tom, then "How will we get it back, it's Saturday tomorrow?"

"Oh, drat," said June, "I never thought of that." Everyone would be home tomorrow: Fran and the two other sets of neighbours. "We'll just have to leave it there until Monday," she said. "I just hope Meghan doesn't notice it on her way over to pick me up tomorrow."

"I doubt she will," said Tom "There are always so many cars along that stretch of the road that she won't notice ours amongst them."

"I hope not," said June. "I get so stressed at having to think fast about us."

Tom laughed, "Well, you're pretty good at it, Beanie, you deserve a BAFTA."

June rolled her eyes at him, thinking this was no joking matter, but then she looked at him and immediately laughed. That was always part of the attraction for her, that he never failed to make her smile. When they got to the road, Tom found a parking space right at the beginning.

"It's a bit of a trot, Beanie, but I'll carry you."

He got out of the car and went round to help her out then he swept her up into his arms and did the walk to their front door. He put her down and opened the door; she hobbled inside. "Come on, Beanie, I'll help you up the stairs." They went up slowly. When they got into the bedroom, June sat on the bed and he undressed her, laying her in bed, he bent forward, stroking her hair looking into her eyes and they kissed. June looked at the clock, it read nine-forty, she began to unbutton his shirt.

"No, Beanie, you're in pain, darling."

"Oh, but I need something to make me feel better," she teased. "Get undressed, Tom, we have time."

He undressed and climbed into bed, kissing her more and more passionately. She pulled him on top of her for something only he could give her.

After he'd gone, she lay with her ankle throbbing but eventually fell into a fitful sleep, dreading tomorrow for the fact she would have to lie to her children and because she was not seeing Tom until late.

CHAPTER 5

June awoke and the first thing she felt was her ankle, still throbbing but nothing like as bad as yesterday, she wondered if being her young self had helped it heal faster. Many questions of this type would come to June while she was going about her day without Tom. She was fascinated by how her mind had retained the normality of her life as a seventy-four-year-old even though her body was a lot younger. She often got caught out by her reflection if they were out and wondered who that was staring at her. This experience was fun but it certainly did have many unanswered questions and puzzling moments.

June got out of bed, tentatively putting her ankle on the floor and slowly standing up. It could definitely take more weight than yesterday, but she still had to walk with a hobble. She pulled the bandage off and saw that it was still very bruised, she would have breakfast before attempting to have a shower, then she would put a fresh support on and get ready to be picked up by Meghan.

She sat ready by ten-thirty, thinking of Tom and missing his presence. She had got used to having him around for those twelve hours but she knew she would have a good day with her family; it would be wonderful to see all three of her children again. The doorbell rang and June got up and opened the door to Meghan.

"All ready, Mum?"

June picked up her handbag and limped out of the door.

"Oh God, Mum, what's wrong?" Meghan asked with a concerned look.

"Oh, nothing really, just a sprained ankle." June tried to make light of it, but she knew her daughter would want all the details and may even insist on a hospital visit.

"How did you do it?"

"I went for my walk yesterday and slipped, that was all."

"Did you go to A&E, Mum?"

"No, it's only a sprain. It just needs rest and

support. Really Meg, I'm fine."

"We'll see how it goes today, Mum, it may need looking at. You really need to be careful with all this walking you know."

"I know," said June ready to pull on Tom's story.

"I stupidly had the wrong shoes on. I usually always wear trainers for my walks but decided to put sandals on. I won't be doing that again in a hurry."

Meg seemed to be part satisfied with this excuse, but had a look that told June she was still concerned. She helped June into the car and drove the few roads to Meghan's house, passing the car that Tom had parked there the night before.

June was so worried about going past it with her daughter she immediately started to talk. "So, Meg, is everyone there yet?"

"Well, Paul's there - alone. I did wonder if he'd turn up with his latest date but apparently, he's giving it a rest for the moment, which is good as he still hasn't got over the

157

divorce, and Jane said she'd get there for twelve - she's getting the train from London so she can have a drink."

"That's nice. I can't wait to see you all, I've missed you."

"We miss you too, Mum, which is why we've made up the spare room for you tonight. We're going to make a weekend of it." June stared straight ahead, she didn't want to stay over, she wanted to come home to Tom.

"Oh no, darling, that's alright, I'm only up the road from you."

"I know, Mum, but you're in that house all on your own now and we thought it'd be nice for you to have some company for a couple of days. We'll take you back Monday morning and now, seeing your ankle, I'm glad you'll be with us. You won't be able to do anything for yourself, so that's made it definite."

June looked out the car window. How could she tell her daughter that she wasn't alone, that she would do hardly anything herself as her husband would be there to wait on her?

She didn't know what to say to Meghan, as to decline too much would seem ungrateful. She was in a quandary, but thought she'd wait until later to bring up the fact that she wanted to go home.

They pulled onto Meghan's drive and went into the back garden.

"Nan!" Samantha shrieked and ran up to her Nan to hug her.

"Careful, Sam," said her Mum, "Nana's hurt her ankle."

"Oh no, Nan, how did you do that?" and she repeated the story of her fall to Sam.

She walked down to the gazebo where Paul, Chris and Meghan's husband David were. They all saw her coming and all asked about her limp, for the third time in an hour she recounted the story, complete with the 'wrong shoes' aspect. They all greeted her with a hug and Paul held her arm taking her over to a chair.

"Sit down, Mum, and rest your ankle," he said, always her little knight in shining armour, even at thirty-seven, always her little boy. They came over to sit with her and talked about Chris and his imminent university admission. He was excited about going and it was his dream to become an architect; this was the first part of the journey.

"We're going to miss him though, aren't we, David?" Meghan said.

Chris looked suitably embarrassed and just said, "You'll get over it, Mum," with a smile.

As they were deep in conversation, they heard Jane's voice as she came through the back gate. "Hello everyone." June wanted to jump up but instead, stood slowly and put her arms out for her younger daughter.

"Jane darling, oh you look wonderful."

June was always struck by the extreme prettiness of Jane, of her delicate features and small, neat figure. Recent experiences had shown June where she got it from: she thought how like Jane she was when Tom visited. Jane had brought wine and some barbecue food, which she took into the kitchen. She came out and joined the group as David lit the barbecue. They continued their conversations on many subjects including Paul's foray into dating. "I'm giving it a rest for now," he said. "I don't exactly know what I'm looking for," he said.

Meghan laughed, "Good, you need to give it a rest. I've got a terrible memory for names and they keep changing."

Paul laughed, "Shall I just always go for ones with the same name, would that help?"

"Yes please, that sounds like a good idea."

The conversation went on in a happy and light way until Jane said to June, "So Mum, how are you coping?"

"Not too bad, sweetheart. It's all a bit strange and different but I spend a lot of time thinking about your father. I do a lot of walking and I still talk to him." June realised the reality of that statement; a reality for her that her children would never know about.

"That's sweet, Mum," Jane replied. "I was going to ask if you were ready to go out yet? There's a few shows that you might want to go and see or I can come and stay with you at weekends now and then."

"That's lovely, Jane, yes, we'll have to go to the theatre. I can stay at yours and go home. It'll be a bit far to travel back after a show, I can come home the next day."

"OK, Mum. Have a look at the shows on at the moment and I'll book one for a couple of weeks' time."

"Thank you, darling," said June to her daughter. "That sounds perfect. I'll have a look and phone you."

June felt a surge of excitement at going out for a night to see a show. She and Tom would do that each year on June's birthday so it would be a wonderful experience to do it again with her daughter.

David emerged from the kitchen with a cool-box full of food. He was wearing an apron with *"King of the Barbecues"* on the front as he got down to the job of providing food to everyone. Samantha had put some music on, wine flowed and everyone seemed to be thoroughly enjoying the day.

Samantha shouted to June, "Nan, it's a shame about your ankle, I know you'd just love to get up and dance."

"I definitely would, Sam, you know me," June laughed.

"I know, Nan, you can certainly bust some moves."

Sam had invited three of her friends who were dancing, they were enjoying themselves like sixteen-year-old girls do when they have all the confidence in the world. June looked at their clothes, it was strange to think how she would want to buy those for herself. She pictured herself wearing what they had on and made a mental note to ask where they shopped. She may only have a week left with Tom but one or two new items wouldn't go amiss. She had been surviving on the same three dresses all week. She started to think about the past week and about how it all began with the visit from Mr James. She still hadn't processed any of it, as it was too surreal to make any sense of. Like Tom said, *don't question it, just enjoy it.* She thought about how passionate they had been together all week and felt guilty that she had not behaved like the grieving widow that everyone thought she'd been, but to have turned down this chance to be a couple again and a young one at that, would have been silly. She would have plenty of time to grieve when this experience was over, then she would be back to being Mum and Nan again.

"You OK, Mum? You're miles away," asked Paul, sitting himself next to June and putting his arm round her shoulder.

"Yes darling, just thinking about Dad and what a good dancer he was. You know how he loved his music."

"Yes, I remember as a kid you and him playing records and dancing with us. He was certainly good, a bit of a looker too, wasn't he?"

"Oh yes, Paul, Dad certainly was," and she thought of the admiring glances he had got in the past week when they had gone out. The waitress at the pub was definitely flirting with him when she took the order, but June had never felt jealous of his effect on women. Tom only ever had eyes for June. He had made her feel so secure during their marriage, she never felt any urge to feel jealousy.

"Do you know, Paul, when I think of your Dad, although I'm sad at not having him here, there is a lot of happiness to remember. We were special, him and me, what we had was special."

"I know, Mum. It was lovely to watch and be around. It was magical for us kids growing up with that amount of positivity and love around. I'm just gutted I couldn't find the same thing."

"Oh Paul, don't beat yourself up. What your Dad and me had was very rare, I know that."

Paul put his hand on top of hers and sat with her, both thinking of Tom.

"You alright you two? asked Meghan.

"Yes, we're fine, Meg," Paul replied, "We were just talking about Dad."

"He was a wonderful Father, wasn't he? And you were a wonderful Mum, too. The pair of you gave us such a great upbringing," said Meghan, continuing, "I've made up the bed for you, Mum, and thought it would be nice for you to stay for a few days."

"Oh no!" June replied quickly. "No, I can't"

"Why Mum?" asked Meg.

June was grappling for something to say, she couldn't consider not seeing Tom for days. "I like being at home, darling, I feel close to your Dad there."

"We just thought that it might be good for you to have some company. We've hardly heard from you this week and when we do see you, you've hurt yourself and there was no one there to help you. We worry, Mum."

"I know darling, but I really can look after myself and I do love my home, you know that." June felt guilty as she looked at Meg, who obviously thought she was helping by asking June to stay.

"OK, Mum," she conceded. "Well, just stay

tonight. We really want to have you around, you know, the kids will love you being here."

June fought with her want to insist on going home but also knew that Tom would want her to accept their daughter's kindness.

"Yes, alright darling, I'll stay tonight then go back tomorrow."

"Of course, Mum, we'll take you back tomorrow evening."

June felt a surge of disappointment. She could not possibly turn down Meghan's offer - her daughter clearly wanted her to be around but, in her heart, June felt a pang of regret that she would have to let go of two days with Tom. He could visit when she got home but it would be later than she would want at the beginning of their last week.

At that moment David called out, "Food!" and there was a general gathering around the barbecue.

Paul stood up and said, "Shall I get you some Mum?"

"Yes please, Paul." She smiled at her son, happy for him to get her some food and give her time alone to process not seeing her husband for a while. The barbecue carried on with its revelry, some neighbours had joined the party. June sat and watched what Tom and she had achieved with the wonderful people around her and she wished he could be here. This is the first time she had had a chance to miss him since the day of the funeral. It felt strange to miss someone so much you had spent a week with, but the missing was based on their fifty years together prior to this strange afterlife experience. She wondered what the children would say to her if she told them, she thought to herself with amusement, they would say she was bonkers no doubt and Meghan would *never* let her leave their house. She couldn't even ask Tom to visit with the children present, he would never appear in front of the children for the reasons Mr James said, so she would just be a batty old Mum.

Samantha came over. "What are you smiling at, Nan?"

"Oh," said June, "I was just thinking of your Granddad."

"Oh, that's so sweet," Meghan said before being dragged to dance by one of her friends who had decided that even though they were surrounded by a load of boring oldies who stood and talked, dancing was the way to go at this barbecue.

Jane came over to sit with June. "You OK, Mum?"

"Yes, Jane and how are you sweetheart? How is work?"

"Oh, you know, stressful. Not easy this week as I had cases that were continuing from before the funeral and I haven't had a chance to miss Dad as much as I would like. I'm going to take some time off soon and just have a week out to myself, get off the treadmill and allow myself to think."

"That's a good idea, Jane, you work so hard."

"All part of being a lawyer, Mum. I'm not sure it was the best career choice but it's what I decided and it pays the bills."

"I know, sweetheart, but you were so happy to get the Law degree, you definitely wanted it very much. What about your social life?"

Jane knew exactly what her Mum was asking. "Well, you'll be pleased to know I'm still with Marcus." Marcus was a lawyer too and Jane had been with him for around four months.

"When are we going to get to meet him?" asked June with a smile.

"Soon, Mum, you know I'm a commitment-phobe, it's a big step meeting the family."

"I know. Does he make you happy darling?"

"Yes Mum, yes he does and he's funny, but I just don't want it to get too intense too quickly, it'll burn itself out."

June thought back to meeting Tom and knowing within a week they would be married, that they wanted to be together forever. Phrases like 'commitment-phobe' just did not exist back then but whatever one of those was, Tom and June were the opposite. Fortunately, it never burned itself out with them, just got brighter with each passing year. June wondered if this was what made a soulmate. "You know, Jane, your Dad and I knew right from the start... we just knew we wanted to be together - it was a feeling, a surety."

"That's what made you and Dad so different though Mum, you were really meant to be. Absolute soulmates."

June was happy that someone else had described them as such, it reinforced the whole experience that was happening right now. They were special and it happened to those that were genuine soulmates, just as Mr James had explained.

"What time are you leaving to go back, Jane? I don't really like the idea of you on public transport too late at night."

"Oh, I'm staying, Mum. Meghan said I can have the sofa and go back tomorrow, so you needn't worry. Also, you're stuck with me for ages yet," and she bumped her mother jokingly. June was glad that she had agreed to stay, as she would get to spend time with both her daughters. Paul would be going home much later by taxi, so he wouldn't have to leave too early. June thought that if she wasn't seeing Tom, being with all of their children was absolutely on a par and began to feel easier about not seeing him for almost two days.

The September evening began to take on its seasonal dampness, making the late summer sun less productive. Meghan lit the garden heater and they knew it wouldn't be long before they had to go in, as the days had become markedly shorter. June was enjoying the company of her family but could not stop thinking about Tom and what they might be doing at this moment. She distracted her sadness by thinking about what they would do on Monday, as tomorrow would be written off for going out anywhere by the time she got home. They could have a meal at home and listen to more of the records that they had been working through all week. She would have liked to go somewhere by train with him, but the memory of their last and fateful planned train journey and what had occurred on the platform meant June was not ready to repeat anything that reminded her of that day.

The rest of the evening was spent indoors with wine, beer, hot chocolate and games like charades, always a firm favourite at Reader family get-togethers. June went to bed earlier than the others: she was exhausted by the events of the past days which no one could even begin to imagine. Paul helped her up to her bedroom and gave her a hug goodbye, as he would book his taxi after a couple more beers and said he would pop in to see her during the week.

"Let me know though, darling, you know what I'm like for going out on my walks," asked June.

"Mum, you can't go walking with that ankle, don't be silly." She was too tired to think of what to say, she would cross that bridge when she came to it.

"You're right Paul, but phone anyway, I can know when to put the kettle on."

"OK, Mum, will do. See you in the week. Love you."

"Love you too," she said, as he kissed her on the cheek and left the room.

Her ankle was still uncomfortable but had lost its incessant throb and as soon as she lay her head on the pillow, she was asleep. Her dreams were fitful and full of visions of Tom. She was confused in her dream - *was he here?* She then found that she could not get near him, every time she reached for him, he began to get further away. All night she had these dreams, waking up spasmodically to learn that she had been dreaming and relieved that tomorrow night, when she reached for him, he would come to her.

She woke early the next morning, the house was silent as everyone was still asleep from their late night. She got out of bed and tested her ankle, still painful but increasingly usable, she managed to limp to the bathroom and quietly showered then went back to the room and dressed. When she was dressed, she went downstairs, creeping past the lounge where Jane was sound asleep. June made herself a cup of tea and wrapping her cardigan round her, went to sit in the garden. If she couldn't be with Tom, she would spend this alone time thinking about him.

After an hour, the rest of the household began to rise, Meghan first, then Jane, who stood looking at June through the window of the kitchen.

"Do you think she's OK?" Jane asked.

"I'm not sure, there's just something about her that doesn't seem to want to let go just yet."

"Does she need to though, Meg?"

"No, maybe not but we need to keep our eye on her. We don't want her getting depressed."

"I agree. I'll make sure I look in on her again this week and let you know how she seems."

"Thanks Meg. It's horrible being so far away

sometimes, by the time I get in from work I'm fit to drop. Sorry it gets left to you."

"Don't be silly, Jane, we're sisters - it's what we do for each other," and she gave Jane a small hug. The girls made tea and went out into the garden to join their mother.

Meghan pointed to the cold and dirty barbecue. "I hope David's up soon; he has a job to do." and they all laughed.

The rest of the day went by in a haze of preparing food, cooking it and the extreme hunger felt when a household has a roast dinner cooking. Samantha and Chris had the usual scrap over laying the table and, as they all sat round eating a delicious meal. Meghan said, "I thought you might like to stay for the evening Mum?"

"I would. darling." said June. "but this late summer is playing havoc with my garden and I'll need to water it before it turns into a desert." June was relieved that this was not actually a lie, but it had the added bonus of being able to see Tom sooner rather than later.

"I can always pop back and put the sprinkler on for you. Mum." said Meghan helpfully.

"No. sweetheart, you have enough to do. You stay and have some me-time... you've earned it."

Meghan was rather relieved at not having to drive back and would indeed be grateful for some time to relax. Chris would be going to university in just over a week and she still had some bits left to get for him. "OK Mum, we'll have dinner, I'll clear up, we can have a cuppa then I'll drive you back."

"Perfect," said June, closing her eyes at the anticipation of seeing Tom and the way it made her feel.

Meghan helped June out of the car and to the front door.

"Oh Mum, are you sure you're going to be OK with that ankle?"

"Yes, honestly, it's getting better by the minute."

"What about the stairs?" Meghan asked with concern.

"I'll be fine, darling; I did your stairs didn't I?"

"Yes, true. Well, if there's anything you need or you decide you want to come back, please just call me Mum - I'll be straight over."

"Of course, I will," June said to her daughter, thinking how lovely she was. "I'll be just fine but yes, if there is anything, I'll phone you, promise."

"OK, Mum."

June kissed Meghan on the cheek, saying, "Now go, go! Go and put your own feet up this afternoon," and she watched Meghan get in her car and drive away.

June walked slowly into the garden. She was able to put weight on her ankle today but didn't want to tempt fate by overusing it. She switched on the sprinkler and went back into the lounge, ready and longing to see Tom. It felt like the first time she had seen him as she stood in her usual clothes, not wanting this time to waste a moment by having to get changed. June knew that when she appeared as a twenty-year-old, she would feel good in a bin-bag; she would change afterwards. Besides, she knew that having not seen Tom yesterday, her clothes may not be on for long, feeling guilty at this thought she told herself silently, *it's what young and in-love couples do.*

Looking at the clock she saw it was four thirty-five, this would mean a late night, with Tom leaving in the early hours but this would be alright, as he would be back tomorrow at 9 am to go and get the car after Fran had left for work. She went over to the record player and placed the needle on the record then, as ever, stood with her eyes closed.

When she heard the words, "Hello, Beanie," her heart skipped and she ran as fast as her ankle would allow and jumped into his arms.

They kissed long and passionately. "Oh Tom. I've missed you."

"Oh, my darling," was all he could say before kissing her again.

As they parted, he stood back and looked at her. "Beautiful," he said, "even in clothes that are two sizes too big."

"I didn't bother to take them off. I just wanted to see you."

"That's alright, Beanie. Shall we go and take them off now?" he said, with a mischievous smile and a wink. He picked her up and carried her up the stairs into the bedroom, where they quickly undressed and fell onto the bed together.

Afterwards, they showered and went downstairs, Tom holding onto her hand. She began to prepare them a meal and they talked about the barbecue.

"How were the children, Beanie" he asked.

"They were fine, Tom. It was a marvellous day. Jane is still with Marcus, but she didn't bring him - you know what she's like with her private life, it's always very private."

"Yes, she was like that as she grew up too, played her cards close to her chest when it came to boyfriends," he laughed.

"Well, she said I will get to meet him soon. Meghan and David are well, although Meg still runs about all over the place like a whirling dervish and Paul, well, to be honest, Paul seemed the best I've seen him since the divorce. Of course, he misses you terribly but I think this is a time that has made him reflect on life."

"Good. He needed to breathe before he fell head-first into another relationship. What did they say about your ankle?"

"They were worried, of course, but as soon as I said about the wrong shoes, which they all told me off about, they seemed happier. I did miss you though, Tom, is that awful? I was with our children but I wanted to be with you."

"No, that's not awful, Beanie. We've only got a limited amount of time I suppose, so you're bound to want to use it all. Don't beat yourself up with guilt about that; if the roles were reversed, I'd feel the same." He kissed her head and she was struck by his total understanding at all times throughout their lives, even when she had post-natal depression after Jane was born. Tom gave such tailored support for her needs and in the awful lows she hit for almost six months afterwards, there was never a moment where she felt she didn't want him around, even through her darkest minutes. *Maybe these things are the indication of a true soulmate*, she thought. They ate their meal, with June continually touching his arm; she needed to know he was really here today, as even just one day wasted had a profound effect on her. She had slipped into one of her little dresses and as she drank the wine Tom had poured her, she felt light and happy.

"Come on," she said, dragging him into the lounge. "Let's play some music," and they sat listening to music.

As the music played, they heard the doorbell. June looked out of the window from behind the net curtains.

"It's Fran!" she said to Tom.

The music was quite loud, Fran was bound to hear it. She rang the doorbell again and lifted the letterbox, calling June's name "June! June!"

Tom and June had sat down under the window, Tom said, "What about the music?" June put her finger on his lips. The doorbell rang again and after a few more minutes June dared to peep over the windowsill, Fran was gone.

They turned the music down. "I'll say I was in the shower," said June.

"You're getting good at these excuses, darling."

"Maybe I'll just tell her I was here with a twenty-three-year-old man; that'll make poor old Fran's hair stand on end."

By now, it was dark and they sat in the conservatory by candlelight. The fox came back to give them one of his shows; it was almost as if he enjoyed walking round the garden for them to admire.

"How can normal be so odd, Tom?" June said about the situation. "I mean, here's you and me, nothing dramatic, nothing fantastical happening, yet this, being here... this in itself is like something so out of this world, it's just amazing."

"I know," replied Tom. "Two people sitting here looking so ordinary but it's the most extraordinary thing anyone could imagine."

"What shall we do tomorrow?" she asked.

"We'll think of somewhere to go. If your ankle isn't too bad, we can walk down and drive somewhere from where we've parked the car. Is it alright there, by the way?"

"Yes, it is. It's strange that Meghan drove by it twice and didn't notice it, but then she has no reason to notice a random car as being her Dad's, thank goodness. That would have taken some explaining."

"Too right," replied Tom. "Well, come on then sleepyhead, let's get you to bed."

"I'm tired but I don't want to sleep Tom, I'll miss you going."

"I'll be back before you know it, Beanie, come on," and he put his hand out and pulled her up.

She awoke at 7 am. Tom was gone. The indent of where his head had been still on the pillow, she placed her head there, wondering what today would bring and marvelling at these two extra weeks for the time they gave her, knowing when this was over, she would not be able to say I love you anymore, or stroke his face, or do any of the little things they enjoyed together. *To be given this extra time goes part way to make up for the sadness of not doing them again.* She was honoured and grateful to whoever or whatever had bestowed this gift upon her, "Thank you" she whispered, hoping it would be heard.

She stood up, resting her weight on her ankle to see how it felt. She felt no pain, so tentatively began to walk, finding that it all seemed fine. She was grateful for this, as she had decided to ask Tom if they could go and visit the place they both lived as youngsters and see how it had changed, if indeed it had. She showered for the first time without any pain in her ankle and as she washed her body, she marvelled yet again at the miracle of what was happening to her, giving her the chance to spend these extra days with Tom.

As she ate her breakfast, she looked out of the window and saw Fran leaving for work at the usual time; this meant June was free to get Tom anytime from now on. It was almost nine o'clock, she knew that any plans they had for today would be started after they had made love. She had put on the cute little pyjamas she had bought for her young self, consisting of a pair of shorts and a vest top. As she put them on after her shower, she realised that, looking at her reflection, she would look far better in them at twenty. As she got up to go and play their song, the phone rang: it was Meghan.

"Hi Mum, I was just ringing to see how your ankle was and whether you needed any shopping?"

"Oh, sweetheart, that really is so kind of you but no, I'm OK for everything. Also, my ankle doesn't hurt at all today, so it's fine for me getting around but I really appreciate you thinking of me."

"That's OK, Mum. What are you going to do today? I worry about you without Dad, you're rattling around in that house all by yourself."

"I'm fine Meg, really. I'll probably do a bit of gardening and as I've said, it's nice to have the time alone to really concentrate on thinking of your Dad - how it was in the old days."

"Alright Mum, but you must tell me if you feel lonely or sad. We always have a bed for you here, even though it's a madhouse at times."

June thanked her daughter for the offer and promised to tell her if she felt at all lonely – something that may happen after these two magical weeks but certainly not for their duration. She put the phone down and headed into the lounge, where she put their song on and closed her eyes; it wasn't long before she heard his voice.

"Hello, Beanie."

She turned round to see him and ran into his arms; they kissed passionately. He put her at arm's length and commented on both her pyjamas and her body, they kissed again and made love on the lounge floor, something she never thought she would be doing in her seventies. Afterwards, she went upstairs and got dressed, putting on flat sandals that she had bought, not wanting to tempt fate that her ankle would start to hurt again.

"How's the foot, darling?" Tom asked as she came downstairs.

"It's much better, Tom, and useable, but if it starts to hurt while we're out I'll let you know."

"OK, Beanie. So, where are we going?"

"I thought it might be nice if we went back to the town we lived in when we met. It'll be fun to see if our estate has changed."

"That's a great idea, darling, where all this began?" and he pulled her to him, kissing her. "So, do we have to go just yet or should we...?" he smiled cheekily at her.

"No, Tom, we're leaving now. You'll just have to wait until we get back," she laughed as she opened the front door.

All was quiet as they left and walked down

the street towards where they had left the car. As they approached it a man was cutting his hedge in a house near where the car was parked. He looked at the young couple, smiled and said, "Good morning."

They replied and got into the car, driving off towards where they used to live many years ago. It would take them about forty-five minutes to get there at a steady pace and with traffic very light, now that the rush hour had gone. As they drove along, they held hands, travelling in silent bliss at being together again. The estate they lived on was on the outskirts of town and had been dotted with forests and fields; they wondered if it would still look the same. As they approached, they were glad to see one of the forests was still there, it held many a magical childhood memory for them, as forests often do. They noticed a lot of the green fields had been replaced by housing and although this was sad, they both realised that things move on and places change. They went to have a look at their respective houses and were pleased to see they were still there but had been modernised and extended. They looked lovely and as the basic architecture was there, seeing them brought back many happy memories. After spending time generally exploring the area, they decided to have lunch in the local pub, the same pub that their parents had used. The same as the houses, the pub had been redecorated to an extremely high standard, with a restaurant area where the old public bar had once been, where men used to play darts and their chatter slowly got louder as the beer flowed through a haze of cigarette smoke. Now, it was a clean and modern area where Tom and June decided to have lunch. The food was glorious: they had real pub fayre, which tasted amazing.

When they had finished eating, they sat holding hands across the table, talking about their family and both feeling sad that the people they spoke about were no longer with them. Tom retold June many tales about his older brother, whom he had adored. He said after Eddie died, he felt more alone than he ever had in his life; even though he had June, he lost someone who had experienced so many life milestones with him. June remembered how Tom had been after losing his brother; he would often sit alone staring out of the window and June was fine to leave him with his thoughts back then. She too felt sad that Eddie had died; he had always been nothing but lovely to June after she met Tom.

"Ready then, Beanie? Shall we go home?"

June looked at her watch: it was already three-fifteen and Tom would have to go at nine so after the journey home, they would only have five hours left, which sounded long but she knew only too well how quickly the time went when they were together, plus Fran would arrive home from work at just after five and they couldn't risk any comings and goings with the car, as Fran might see them.

"OK, Tom, I've had such a lovely day," and as they walked out of the pub, she kissed his cheek.

They drove home in silence, both just satisfied with being together.

When they got home, they showered together and made love. As they lay together afterwards, Tom stroked June's cheek and hair and marvelled at her beauty. He also knew that he had felt the same about her as they got older together, but seeing her now at twenty, he knew why he had never wanted to let this beautiful woman go once they had met. June looked at him and they kissed. They got up and dressed then went downstairs to have a glass of wine and listen to music together. As June poured their wine she suddenly said, "Oh drat."

"What's the matter, Beanie?"

"I've just realised I left my handbag in the car. I must have been in a hurry to get indoors with you," she smiled.

"I was quite keen too," he said, standing next to her and kissing her neck. "Don't worry, darling, I'll get it for you."

As he opened the front door, he was just in time to see Fran raise her hand to ring the doorbell. Tom was taken aback, as was Fran.

"Hello," she said enquiringly, wondering who this was in June's house.

"Oh hello," Tom replied and promptly stuck out his hand. "I'm Toby, June's gardener."

"Oh, hello... is June in?"

"No," replied Tom, "She had to go out."

"Oh," replied Fran, obviously wondering what the gardener was doing inside June's house while she wasn't there.

Tom thought quickly. "It's OK though Fran, she lets me have access to use the house for loo breaks and making a cuppa."

"Right." Fran still didn't look convinced. "Do you know what time she'll be back?"

"No," said Tom, "but she said it would be after I've left, so maybe you'd be best to come back later or leave a note."

"Yes, I'll pop back later. If she comes back before you go, let her know I've called in."

"Of course, Fran, no worries."

Fran started to walk away but then turned to Tom. "How did you know my name?" she asked.

"You told me when you introduced yourself."

"Did I?" said Fran, having no recollection of telling this man her name. She carried on walking, looking back now and then, as Tom closed the door. He went into the kitchen to see June taking a large sip of wine. "Goodness, Tom, that was close."

"Tell me about it, Beanie. I could have kicked myself when I used her name."

"Well, you seem to have handled it OK, so I'll just have to persuade her that my gardener has the run of the house and I'm happy about it."

He pulled her to him and kissed her passionately.

"You can tell her I have the run of the house and that I'm a really good kisser." They both laughed and spent the evening listening to music until it was almost time for Tom to go. He reached for her and began to undress her;

they liked to make love before he went.

The next morning June got up and still felt warm from Tom's lovemaking the night before. She showered and dressed and as she went downstairs, the doorbell rang. It was Fran.

"Hi June, I'm just off to work but wanted to make sure you were OK."

"Yes," June replied, aware that the conversation was going to involve "Toby" the gardener.

"I called in yesterday but you were out. Your gardener answered the door – Toby I think his name is?"

"Oh yes, he's a great gardener."

"Is it wise for him to have the run of the house while you're not in, June?"

"Yes, of course. I've known him years."

"OK, June, that's fine. I just thought it best to check. He did look familiar to be honest, where does he live?"

"I'm not sure."

"Oh right, I thought you'd known him

years?" Fran felt there was something June wasn't telling her. The young man did look amazingly comfortable wandering around someone else's home.

"Yes, he lives locally."

"I could do with a gardener – you'll have to give me his number."

"Yes, I'll dig it out for you Fran."

Fran left to go to work and June breathed a sigh of relief. As she began to think about preparing to see Tom, the phone rang. It was Meghan. "Hi Mum, how are you? How's the ankle?"

"Oh, hello darling, yes, the ankle's all good now and I'm feeling absolutely fine."

"Thank goodness it's better. I was still worrying about it."

"That's sweet, I'm so lucky to have you all. So, how are you and the family? It was lovely to see you all at the weekend."

"Yes, we're all good Mum. Chris is almost ready for university; I'm going to miss him."

"You will," replied June, knowing how close

Meg was with her son.

"Anyway, what I wondered Mum, is whether you can come over on Thursday and stay with the kids. David and I are thinking about going away for a couple of days for his birthday. We would leave Thursday afternoon and be back no later than teatime on Friday. We want to book a really lovely little restaurant and overnight stay at a cosy inn."

June was taken aback by the question, she quickly worked out in her head that she and Tom could still spend time together on those two days, she was into her final week with him so didn't want to give up any time whatsoever.

"Is there a problem Mum?" Meghan asked, realising June was hesitating in giving a reply. "I know the children don't need babysitting but I'd feel happier knowing that both they and the house were being looked after, but if it's not convenient...?"

"Oh, don't be silly, sweetheart, it's absolutely fine. I'm more than happy to do it."

"I'll pick you up on Thursday at one o'clock

Mum, we'll be leaving about two."

"Yes of course Meg, I'm only too happy to help. You and David need some time alone, you both work so hard."

"Ah, thanks Mum. See you Thursday."

After she put the phone down, June went into the lounge and put their song on, closing her eyes until she heard the now familiar young voice of her Tom.

"Hello Beanie, have you missed me?"

June opened her eyes to see him smiling and she ran into his arms as he scooped her off the floor, swinging her round.

"Oh Tom, I've missed you like mad." They kissed and went upstairs to make love. Afterwards they showered together, enjoying each other and making love again under the cascading water.

"What are we doing today, Beanie?" asked Tom as they got dressed.

"I don't know Tom, is there anything you fancy?"

"You," he said with a cheeky grin.

"Apart from that," laughed June.

"It's another scorcher, Beanie, how about we go for a picnic?"

"That's a lovely idea Tom. I'll put some sandwiches together then we can stop at a supermarket for a few bits."

June got a blanket out of the cupboard and made a few sandwiches. Tom watched her, still marvelling in her beauty. When she had finished and put the sandwiches into a bag, they went to the car and drove toward a country park that was about half an hour from where they lived. They stopped at a supermarket on the way and got a good selection of food and drink.

They made their way to the park and walked through the entrance and along a wooded path that brought them out to a large expanse of green, where there were only a few people enjoying the sun on a working and school day. June spread the blanket on the ground and they sat down, initially just looking around and enjoying being together. June told Tom about her house-sitting coming up for Meghan but insisted that she would still see Tom.

"Don't worry Beanie, the children come first so you must never let us get in the way."

"It's not that Tom, it's just that we don't have many days left and I don't want to waste this blessing we've been given. I can do things for the kids any time after our time together, for now I want the chance to be with you."

"I understand darling" said Tom "I do feel the same way too but I wanted you to know whatever you choose is fine with me."

"I do love you, Tom," she said, leaning toward him for a kiss. He kissed her and pulled away saying, "Oh dear, Beanie, we'd better eat before I get too carried away on this blanket."

June laughed and jokingly smacked his arm. They ate and drank and afterwards June lay with her head in Tom's lap while he gently stroked her hair. June began to fall into a half sleep state, being aware of the smell and feel of her lovely husband close to her. Tom looked down at the gorgeous woman with him, he looked at her legs and her body under the light cotton dress that clung to her, he wanted to kiss her all over but was aware they were in a public place, it was difficult for him to resist the urge to touch her. Instead, he carried on stroking her head and enjoying the feeling washing over him of pure contentment and joy. As they made their way home, got in, enjoyed each for the rest of the day and stayed in bed for the evening until Tom was there no more, neither of them could have known that this would be their last day together: both unaware of the catastrophe that was about to hit the family and the sadness it would bring.

CHAPTER 6

June was woken up by the phone ringing, she looked at the clock, it was 1 am. Tom had gone. She hurried downstairs to answer the phone and heard David's distressed voice on the other end. He sounded like he was crying.

"David, what on earth is wrong?"

"Oh June," he said softly, "it's Chris."

"What?" asked June, as she felt her blood run cold.

"He's been in an accident, June. He's in hospital. He's in a coma. We're with him now."

June was trying to process what she had just been told and her first thought was for her darling daughter. "Is Meg with you?"

"Yes. She's sitting in with him now. Oh June, I don't know what we'll do if we lose him."

"You won't, David, he's in the best place. What happened?" June asked.

"He'd gone out with his mates for a drink before he has to go to uni and the car they were in came off the road."

"Who was driving," asked June. "How many were in the car?"

"There were four of them. They've all been injured but Chris came off worst. The driver said it wasn't his fault; a tyre blew, there was nothing he could do. They breathalysed him though, but he hadn't had a drop to drink as he was the designated driver. The poor kid's blaming himself but there was nothing he could have done. Oh June, I don't know what we'll do if we lose Chris."

"David, are you in Queen's?" June asked. That was the hospital closest to them and was a large main hospital with A&E, along with many other departments.

"Yes," David replied.

"OK, I'm going to get a taxi and come to you both."

"Are you sure, June? I think Meg would be grateful to see you right now and we have Sam here too, who's also beside herself."

"Yes, I'll be with you soon."

June put the phone down and immediately phoned for a taxi, which was with her within fifteen minutes, giving her time to get dressed and tidy herself up. She felt numb at what she had just been told: her darling grandson lay in a coma; all his hopes and dreams lay shattered around him just at this moment. The taxi arrived and June got into the back, the driver was sensitive to the fact that June was going to a hospital and did not try and strike up a conversation, instead concentrating on getting her there as quickly and smoothly as possible. The driver pulled up outside the main entrance of the hospital, June paid him and hurried into Reception. David had told her to ask for Intensive Care and to tell them she is a relative. The man on reception was kind, he gently told her where the lifts were and what floor the ICU was. She thanked him for his kindness and made her way to the lifts. When the door opened, she saw another reception area, where she told them who she was and who she was there to see. A nurse asked June to follow her, typing a number into the keypad next to the door, which she opened and smiled kindly at June to go through. The nurse came with her and silently walked June to a room, gently opening the door and telling June her family were in there. June thanked the nurse and went into the room, where immediately Meg ran into her mother's arms, crying, closely followed by Sam. David remained seated by the bed, which June looked at and saw her beloved grandson, lying in a mass of tubes and wires, machinery beeping beside him and his eyes closed. He looked just like he was asleep; there were no marks or blood on him. June could not believe this boy was not about to wake up and tell them all not to worry.

"It's bad Mum," Meghan said. "He's got some swelling on the brain. They don't know if he's going to pull through and if he does, they don't know if there'll be permanent damage. Mum, I can't believe this is happening, he went out so happy that he was seeing his friends for a drink, before leaving them all and going to uni.

I can't bear this pain," and Meg broke down again, her face contorted in misery as tears streamed from her eyes.

June hugged her daughter, becoming aware of how Sam's pretty face was streaked with tears for the brother she argued incessantly with, but loved more than words could say.

"Come here, Sammi," June said and hugged her, together with Meghan, not knowing what to say but knowing that her presence was all they needed right now. David sat stroking Chris's hand and talking to him, gently telling him to please get through this, because he had so many jobs for his son to do before he left them to go to uni. This touched June so much that David was trying so hard to be the one who was holding it together for their family, at that moment June adored her son-in-law more than she ever had before. They all sat round the bed just watching Chris, all willing him to wake up, which did not happen, instead nurses came in frequently to check the machinery.

"How long are we allowed to stay?" asked June, aware that there may be rules in place, even for people in ICU.

"David and I can stay as long as we want. We're to press the alarm if there's any obvious change," Meg said.

"Shall I take Sam home? We can get a taxi back to yours. That'll leave you and David to watch over him."

"No Nan, no, I want to stay," Sam said, through tears.

"Sammi, sweetheart," Meg said, "maybe you and Nanna can go home, you can both get some rest and Dad and I will phone if there's any change, honestly."

"I don't want to leave him, Mum."

"I know, Sammi," David said, "but you and Nan can come back in the morning, after you've had some sleep. I'll come and get you, yes?"

"OK, Dad. I won't sleep though, but promise me I can come in the morning?"

"Of course, my darling, I promise," David

said, cuddling his daughter and silently crying into her hair.

June and Sam left the room, walking back down the corridor and out of the door to the reception area. June asked the kind nurse who had taken her through to ICU if they had the number of a taxi. The nurse smiled softly at June and insisted she would phone on their behalf. The nurse came off the phone and said the taxi would be ten minutes and for them both to wait outside the main entrance. The taxi arrived and they silently got in, June with her arm around her granddaughter all the way home, as Sam cried on and off for the whole journey.

When they got inside the house, June asked whether she should make them both a cup of tea.

"Yes, please Nan."

June made the tea and they sat drinking it. Sam suddenly said, "Nan, I argued with him."

"What, before he went out, sweetheart?"

"Yes. I told him that everything always had

to be about him because he's going to uni. I said that I wished I didn't have a stupid brother. Oh God, Nan, I feel like I've made this happen."

"Oh, Sammi, sweetheart, come here." June put her granddaughter's head on her shoulder. "You two were always arguing – don't forget your brother can be as cutting as you in an argument, but do you know what? Despite all the rows, you two loved each other more than anything, anyone could see that. What has happened to Chris had absolutely nothing to do with you or what you said. You must stop feeling guilty because he loved the arguments and so did you – it was a sign of a happy family. Your Mum used to argue with Auntie Jane all the time and then Uncle Paul came along and they would both gang up on him, but our house was always a home and a happy one, the same as yours is. We just need to Chris to come through this and be around for a few more arguments with his sister."

"Thank you, Nan," said Sam, taking her

Nan's hand. "I love you so much and I really miss Granddad right now."

"Me too sweetheart, me too," said June. It was the first time that she had been made aware that while their grandson lay in the hospital, her and Tom would have no more days of fun and laughter, family came first and he would be in total agreement with that. Their magical two weeks had been cut short but June didn't care about anything but getting Chris better. Her life was secondary and they had had over a week together, enjoying each other's company but now, something had come along which needed all of June's focus and if Tom were here, he'd say that too.

"Nan, can we sleep down here tonight? I don't want to be on my own."

"Of course we can, sweetheart. Go and get your pyjamas on and if you've got some of your Mum's I can borrow?"

"Yes of course." Sam disappeared upstairs, coming back down a moment later wearing her pyjamas and she handed a pair to June. June went upstairs to wash her face and put the pyjamas on that Sam had found for her. When she came down Sam had transformed the sofa into a sofa bed and was sitting crying, June climbed onto the bed to be next to her granddaughter and held her.

"Oh sweetheart," she said, "I'm so sorry," and began to cry with Sam.

Eventually, Sam lay her head down and June watched her fall asleep. What a horrible day it had been. June thought of Tom and how much she needed him but knew there was no way she would be able to see him while their grandson lay in hospital in a coma. Their daughter would need June to be there for her. She knew at that moment she may never see Tom again but her overriding wish was for Chris to recover and for their family to feel happiness instead of the despair they felt right now. June lay down next to Sam and tried to sleep. She closed her eyes but could not stop thinking of Chris and how it would be if the worst were to happen. The thought was too painful to bear so June got up and made a cup of tea, all the time willing her grandson to pull through. June went back to bed, where she eventually fell asleep and her dreams were full of Tom and Chris. Tom was calling out to Chris but Chris couldn't hear him. She woke with a start with the telephone ringing, Sam ran to the phone. June heard her say, "Mum, how is he?" then watched her face as she looked despondent and sad, June was afraid of what was being said and gestured to Sam.

"Mum," she said, "Nan's here, do you want to speak to her?" Sam handed the phone to June.

"Hello Meg, how is he?"

"No change, Mum" she replied, "They say that it could be days weeks or even months with deep comas, but the main thing is that he's still alive, Mum. He's still with us."

"Oh yes, Meg, that's what we must hold on to. He could wake up from this and be the same old Chris. Have they said anything about that?"

"Well, they said that it's impossible to say at the moment. His brain is swollen, but when the swelling goes, everything could be absolutely fine, so we're just keeping our fingers crossed."

"That's good, darling. Do you want me to come to the hospital so you and David can come home for a bit?"

"Oh yes, Mum, that would be good. We can just have a shower and freshen up at least, then come back."

"What about sleep, darling, are you tired?"

"We slept in the chairs last night next to his bed, so we're not too bad but we would appreciate a shower and change of clothes."

"OK Meg, I'll get a taxi. What about Sam, shall I tell her to get ready for school?"

"She's fine to stay off at the moment Mum. Bring her with you to the hospital if you want, as they said it would be good to keep talking to him and I know he'd love to hear her voice."

"Yes, of course Meg, we'll be with you shortly."

June told Sam to get ready as they were going to the hospital. Sam ran upstairs to get ready quickly and June went into her daughter's bedroom to freshen up and get dressed. June phoned for a taxi and they got to hospital, making their way to the Intensive Care Unit where they found a tired and worried Meghan and David. June hugged them both.

Sam went to her brother's bedside and said, "Hello you, I bet you've missed me, haven't you? Actually, I bet you haven't," and she put her hand over his. There was no response from Chris but Sam continued to chatter away to him as they all hoped for some kind of movement, however small.

"Mum, I'm so scared," Meghan said to her mother.

"I know, darling, I know. What do the doctors say?"

"They said they won't know much until the swelling goes down. They've sedated him to keep him in a coma as apparently, this will give the brain more chance to recover."

"How long will that be for?" asked June.

"They don't know. They're going to keep looking at his brain with a CT scan and as soon as it shows enough shrinkage, then they'll stop sedating him."

June watched as Meg's face contorted in pain as she began to silently cry.

"Oh darling, come here," and she wrapped her arms around her child. "You and David go home and I'll phone you immediately if there's any change. Get into some fresh clothes and if you need a lie down, I'm here and won't leave Chris alone for one moment."

They both looked at him as he lay there, and apart from the machinery and tubes, he still just looked asleep. This comforted Meg, her boy was just asleep and while he slept, he was repairing; she knew it. Samantha was stroking her brother's hand, still talking to him about anything she could think of.

They both heard her say, "Nice one Bruv, I haven't had to go to school today and it's a double maths, I love you for that." Hearing this, both June and Meghan couldn't help a smile at his lovely sister, just being herself with Chris, knowing this would indeed be what he would want and need.

"Do you want me to speak to Jane and Paul?" asked June, thinking that Meg would want her siblings at a time like this.

"It's OK, we rang them this morning just before you got here. They're devastated, Mum."

Chris was so close to his auntie and uncle, particularly Paul, who shared his passion for rugby. Paul would often take Chris to local games, where they would cheer and shout unheard advice to the players. Afterwards, they would go for what Paul would call a "dirty burger" and come home late in the afternoon, still buzzing about the rugby match and continuing to talk rugby for what seemed like an age to Meghan. David was more than grateful to Uncle Paul for sharing Chris's love of rugby, being more of a football man himself.

"They're coming later, Mum. Jane's finishing work early and picking Paul up from work on her way. They should be here about one o'clock but David and I will be back by then. I can't bear to leave him for long, Mum."

"Of course not, sweetheart, that's fine. Sam and I will stay with you all. I'll take Sam for something to eat a bit later when you get back. They have a café downstairs in this hospital - we can get her something there."

"Thanks Mum," said Meg, hugging her Mum and feeling the darkest she had ever felt.

After Meghan and David had left, June sat the other side of Chris's bed and watched his sister gently talking to him about school and some of her friends.

"Just to let you know that Kirsten is fine, you know Chris – Kirsten, the pretty one that you have a thing for," Sam laughed, then said "Oh it's OK, Bruv, Nanna's here but she's cool with secrets, aren't you Nan?"

"Of course I am, you two should know that by now. Your secret crush is safe with me, Chris. We just need to get you better and out of here and you'll be seeing her again."

June sat with her hand on Chris's arm, marvelling at the lovely relationship these two siblings had and feeling like she would give anything to bring her grandson back to them. For two hours June and Sam spoke to each other and to Chris, until Meg and David returned.

"Any change?" Meg asked, as she entered the room.

"No, sweetheart," said June, "but you said he was in an induced coma, so I don't think there will be much change until they take him off the drugs, but it's this rest that is giving him a chance to heal."

"Yes, I guess so, Mum."

"We've been talking almost non-stop though, Meg. He knows he's never alone and I think that's the main thing for now."

"Yes, Mum, you're right," and she bent down avoiding the wires and tubes to kiss Chris on the cheek and stroke it. "I'm here Chris and Dad's here too," and she looked at David with sadness on her face. "Mum, do you and Sam want to go and get a cuppa or something, have a little break?"

"Sam?" asked June, "Do you want a cup of tea downstairs?"

"Yes please, Nan," answered Sam.

When they got to the café, June took Sam's hand. "Are you OK, sweetheart? This is so horrible for you."

"I'm alright Nan, I just want Chris to get better. I can't bear it without him, our family would be a mess."

June stroked her granddaughter's hair and after they had got their tea, they sat in silence drinking it.

They went back upstairs to find Jane and Paul in the corridor talking to Meghan. June kissed them both.

"Oh Mum," said Paul.

"I know Paul. Have you been in to see Chris?"

"Yes, very briefly, as they don't like too much disruption on the ICU ward, which makes sense. We're going to go back to Meg's and stay tonight."

"Will you stay too, Mum?" asked Meg.

"Of course I will. I just need to pop home and grab some bits."

"I'll take you, Mum. We'll got to Meg's first and Paul can stay there while we go to yours."

"OK, Jane."

June was so happy to have all her children around her at such a time, and Meghan needed her siblings too. David was an only child and often envied Meg her close family, but they had welcomed him so warmly into the fold that Meg's siblings became like his. There were many times he had been grateful for this and at such an awful time, it felt good to have them around.

"What about you Sammi, do you want to come with us?" asked June, thinking it would be nice for her granddaughter to spend time with her aunt and uncle.

"I'll come with you, Nan. Mum..." she turned to Meghan. "You will let us know as soon as anything changes, won't you?" she asked.

"Of course I will, sweetheart, straight away."

They left and drove home solemnly, dropping off Paul and Sam, then Jane and June carrying on to June's. They went in and June went upstairs to pack a few things.

As Jane walked into the kitchen, then the lounge, she was reminded of many happy times spent in this home, where her Mum and Dad always made them happy. Even through the teenage years when they had to be sullen with their parents, they found it hard to sustain their angst with their Mum and Dad, as they were always such good parents. Their marriage was happy and Jane often thought this was part of the reason for her own avoidance of commitment – she felt unable to ever find what her parents had. If one day she did, then she would jump in with both feet, but so far, she had not met anyone who fulfilled her as much as her Mum and Dad did each other.

Upstairs, June was busily putting things into a small suitcase, when she came across the dresses hanging up that she had worn on her recent dates with Tom. She felt a sudden sadness at not seeing him again, as she knew the next few days, which would have been their last, would have been filled with moments of happiness. Instead, now she was alone and in sole charge of taking care of her family's emotions. She held one of the dresses to her face and could still smell his smell on it, where he had held her.

"Oh Tom," she whispered, "I do so miss you, darling. I really wish you were here," and a tear rolled down her cheek. She quickly folded the dress and put it in the case so that she could at least take a little bit of him with her.

As she came down the stairs, she saw Jane looking at a record, it was the one that had been on the player, their song. "What's this, Mum?"

"Oh, it was Dad and I's song, I play it sometimes when I'm thinking of him."

"That's sweet, Mum. You really miss him, don't you?"

"Yes Jane, especially now, with this going on. He was so much better at dealing with things than me."

"Nonsense, Mum, you were both amazing and that's what he would say to you now; that you're amazing and can get the family through this."

"Oh Jane, I'll try, I really will, but I'm so scared. I won't admit that to Meg at the moment, it's not what she needs to hear."

"I know what you mean, Mum, I'm scared too. I can't even bear to let my thoughts go to a place where Chris didn't get better. He's got to, Mum."

"He will, sweetheart, that's what we must say right now. How was Paul on the drive down?"

"Not good, Mum. Chris was like the son he never had. He's sad, but angry too. He was raging about the boy who was driving, even though Meg had said it wasn't Ben's fault, but I think he just needed to be angry."

"Meg and David have spoken to Ben's

parents; they're absolutely broken-hearted. There was nothing Ben could have done and the police said the same thing. A tyre blew and Ben couldn't control the car. It was virtually a new car too, so it's not like he was driving an old banger. It was just one of those cruel, cruel things and Meg and David are at peace with Ben and his family."

"I know," said Jane. "But you know what Paul's like, heart on his sleeve and all that, he lets his emotions speak too much sometimes. You can have a word, Mum, and calm him down. It was just one of those tragic accidents that happen for no earthly reason and has left our family in bits."

They drove back to Meghan's and went in to find Paul and Sam chatting about Sam's school and what her future plans were.

"Hi Nan," Sam put her arms out to beckon June to her. She put her arms around June's waist. "I'm so glad you're staying. I couldn't do this without you."

"You don't have to, sweetheart, and I think

you've got Aunty Jane and Uncle Paul here for a few days too.

"Yes," they both said together.

"I've spoken to work and I've booked a week off," said Paul.

"Me too," said Jane, who was a junior partner in a legal firm. "I'm not planning on going back for at least a week."

"Thank you, both of you; we all need each other at a time like this."

"Shall I cook us some tea?" asked Jane. "I know we may not feel especially hungry but we do need to keep our strength up. If there is any change, we can just down tools and go to the hospital."

"Yes, good idea," said June, "I'll help."

They all went into the kitchen, where Jane and June found ingredients for spaghetti bolognaise. They all sat down to eat. It was such a contrast to the last time they had all been together at the barbecue, which had been a fun-filled day, where Chris had been full of life and laughed and joked with them all, getting excited about his upcoming university adventure. They all ate what they could and as June loaded the dishwasher, the phone rang. Sam rushed to pick it up. They all listened intently to one half of a conversation, Sam saying, "Yes," "Of course," and "OK," at various times. This told them nothing and as soon as she came off the phone, they were all equally keen to know what had been said.

"That was Dad. He said that he and Mum want to come home to freshen up; they can go back later but they're not allowed to stay overnight again. They asked if you could go to the hospital, Nan, to sit with Chris until they get back?"

"Yes, of course I will."

"Can I go with you, Mum?" Paul asked. He looked at Jane. "Are you alright with that, Jane?"

"Yes, no problem."

"I'll stay here with Aunty Jane," said Sam. "Dad said only two people were allowed at a time."

"OK, sweetheart, I'll be back soon." June gave her granddaughter a hug, saying, "Stay strong, sweetheart."

June and Paul drove to the hospital which was about forty minutes away. After a while into the drive, Paul said, "What's going to happen to the idiot that was driving?"

"Paul, it wasn't his fault at all. I felt like you at first, but Meg and David have spoken to Ben and his parents and the police too. It was a freak accident - a blow-out. Please don't be angry with an eighteen-year-old boy who was doing nothing wrong. Think how this must be making him feel right now."

"I don't really care how he feels, to be honest."

June was shocked. When did her son become like this?

"Paul, stop it, it's not helping anyone." But she could see he was still unreasonably angry with Ben. June hoped they would not have occasion to run into Ben or his parents when Paul was around, as apparently, Ben was in quite a bad way mentally.

They arrived at the hospital and went up to the ward. Chris still lay there surrounded by tubes and beeps. There was a nurse attending to him - the same one as yesterday. She smiled at June and Paul when they came in.

"How is he?" Paul asked.

The nurse looked at June, "You're Nan, aren't you?" then questioningly at Paul.

"Oh, yes, sorry, I'm Paul, his uncle, his mother is my sister."

"OK, Paul," said the nurse. "We'll add you to his visitor list. Intensive Care does have a rather open-door policy but only to family members or in the absence of family, close friends. Only two at a time and mobile phones to be on silent. I know your Nan knows all this but I need to run through it with you. Also, if we are attending to Chris for any reason, we will ask you to wait outside. Sorry there are so many rules, Paul, but the people in this unit are very ill and vulnerable. If you are at all unwell, we would also ask that you do not visit, so that there will be no risk of infection. Well, that's about all so now I'll let you both get on with your visit. Please talk to him. We have sedated him but we know that he can hear you. We'll update his parents about going forward when they come back later but for now, there is no change."

"Thank you, Nurse," June said.

Paul sat beside his nephew and put his hand over Chris's. "Hello mate," he said, with tears in his eyes. "What you been up to, eh? Looks like we need to get you better for them rugby matches we need to go to." Paul's eyes were welling up looking at Chris. He had never seen his nephew so still, so helpless and it was a difficult thing to watch.

"Nan said you need a haircut. She's not into man buns. Don't worry, kid, I won't let her near your hair while you're in here then. When you're awake, you can fight your own corner on that one."

Paul was struggling to find things to say that he felt would not upset Chris. He wanted to talk about university and sport, but he felt these are the things he could never be guaranteed to do again, as they did not know what level of ability and understanding Chris would have when he woke up. Paul thought how different it was in the films, where they had plenty to say and the people woke up amazingly well and right back to themselves. This is not something the medical staff could guarantee until the brain had not only decreased its swelling, but the final answer on whether the injuries Chris sustained would have any lasting repercussions would only be known when he woke up. Paul continued to talk about himself, his work, how he had been determined to give the dating scene up, until the other night, when he met someone from the gym. They then sat in relative silence for the last hour, with Paul occasionally talking about sports results and the television programme Top Gear, which they both loved.

While he was talking, the nurse came in and told them quietly that Meghan had arrived with her sister and that Paul and June would have to leave now due to the two-person rule.

"Of course," replied June and bent down, avoiding the wires, and kissed Chris on the cheek. "Goodbye, Chris," she said, "we'll be back tomorrow to see you."

After they left the ward, they were in the outer corridor, which had a small reception area, they saw Meghan and Jane.

"Hi Mum," said Meghan. "How is he?"

"No change, sweetheart, but they said they'll be talking to you about treatment so maybe you can ask when you're in there?"

"Thanks Mum, I will. Are you ready for this, Jane?" she asked her sister. "It's not going to be a nice experience. Are you alright, Paul?" she asked her brother.

"It's so sad, Meg, I'm so sorry," and he reached out to hug his sister, they were both crying.

"Mum?" said Meg. "David and Sam are at home. David said he was going to come here in about an hour to give Jane a chance to see

Chris. "Are you alright to do Sam and the others some tea? There's food in the freezer or if you need anything, maybe one of you could go to the supermarket?"

"Yes, of course, Meg, don't worry about things like that. We'll just see you and David later; I'll do some sandwiches for when you come home."

"Thanks, Mum," Meg kissed her, then June and Paul left the hospital to go back to Meghan's.

They got back and it was not long before David left for the hospital. June started to prepare something to eat, knowing that it would not be long before Jane got back. When she eventually did, her face was tear stained and she went straight to June for a hug.

"Oh darling," said June.

"Mum, I'm so scared, I didn't expect him to be so poorly."

"I know, sweetheart, it is a shock."

June finished cooking and they all sat solemnly round the dinner table, eating the meal June had put together.

"This is delicious, Nan, thank you." They all agreed with Sam; they just wished they were eating a meal in better circumstances. As they finished and were getting up to go into the lounge to watch something distracting on television, the phone rang. Sam ran to it.

"Hello," she said anxiously. "Yes, but is he OK, Mum?" followed by "OK," and held the phone out to June. "She wants to speak to you, Nan. Chris is fine, there's no change."

"Hello, Meg," said June quietly.

"Hi, Mum. Just to fill you all in. They are going to take Chris off the sedatives tomorrow as the brain swelling has stopped, so they think the induced coma may have done its job of helping him heal."

"That's good to hear, Meg."

"Well, it is and it isn't. The hours after he comes off sedation are critical to know whether he has the ability to wake up himself, and if he does, it will also start to determine whether we have the old Chris back or not. We're still really scared, Mum."

"Be strong, both of you. We'll deal with anything we have to, just as long as we get Chris back."

"I know, Mum, that's what we've said. Anyway, I also wanted to tell you that we've booked ourselves into a Travel Lodge literally five minutes away, so that we can just be with him in a moment. I'm popping home later to get some bits together."

"Alright, sweetheart, I'll let the others know. Paul and Jane said they would be staying all week. I don't know what you want to do about Sam and school?"

"I've spoken to school. She won't be going this week at all and next week, we can review things, but at the moment, I want his sister to be available all the time for him if he wakes and asks for her."

"Of course, Meg. I'm here to look after everybody but if you need any of us, please, you must ask. We can be there in no time with anything you need or with just ourselves."

"Thanks so much, Mum. Tell the others I'll see them later and fill them in with what I've just said. Love you, Mum."

When June put the phone down, she was aware of everybody looking at her, eagerly waiting to hear what had been said. June ran through the conversation with them.

Sam said optimistically, "So he'll wake up soon, Nan?"

"Very likely, Sam, but they can't tell for sure. We'll have to wait and see, but be assured if he does, we'll get you there straight away."

"Thanks, Nan. I just know he's going to be alright." Jane put her arm around her. She wanted to share her niece's hope but had the trepidation of an adult, thinking of what Meghan had said about whether they would get the old Chris back and that it was impossible to know until he woke up.

They spent the day chatting, watching daytime television and eating the lunch that June had prepared for them all. Just after lunch, Meghan arrived home to pack up some bits for her and David for their stay at the hotel. They were all pleased to see her and all thought how tired and drained she looked: the emotional turmoil was taking its toll and June hated seeing her daughter go through something so devastating.

"Mum!" shouted Sam as Meg came through the door and ran to cuddle her. "Is there any change?"

"No, sweetheart, Nan told you what was going to happen, yes?" she asked.

"Yes. He'll wake up soon won't he, Mum?"

"Well, we don't know for sure but it's highly likely. I'll phone as soon as he does, and someone will bring you." She looked at everyone and they all eagerly agreed that they would.

After Meghan had left, they carried on with trying to distract themselves and each other any way they could, paying particular attention to Sam, who was excited about what tomorrow would bring. Sedation was being withdrawn first thing tomorrow, Chris waking up would happen sometime throughout the day and their sense of fear and hope was tangible. Paul insisted on using the internet to read as much as he could on brain injuries and, after watching an evening of television, they went to bed, exhausted from worry.

As June lay in bed, she thought of how much she needed Tom right now. Doing this without him was so difficult, as he was always such a rock to them all. They were all feeling his loss but none more than June, who had lost her life partner, the one that could always steady their family, who had words of wisdom and great big shoulders to bear his family's load on.

June said out loud, "Oh, Tom, I really need you."

She thought of the last days she had spent with him, how they were young and how the whole thing seemed like a dream now, but she knew it had not been. She knew that the miracle they had been granted really did happen, but she now thought she needed her

Tom, the old Tom, the one that was the same age group as her, the one that would help her and their children cope with all this. She got up and pulled the dress out of the suitcase, where she had left most of her clothes, and put it to her nose. She could still smell him; she could still feel the magic of being with her husband. She could not see him again, as taking twelve hours out was an impossibility; Chris could wake up at any moment. June was aware that their fortnight together was over in two days so she would not see him again. She felt sad for herself but mainly felt sad for Meghan, that she did not have her father at a time when she really needed him. She closed her eyes and fell into a fitful sleep that was full of dreams of Meghan calling for Chris and begging June to help her find him, as she had lost him.

In the darkness, June became aware of somebody stroking her hair, this a part of the dream she liked as it calmed her. Slowly, June's mind began the adjustment of waking, or at least she felt she was waking. She was swimming in the post-dream state of confusion, until she began to realise that this was real, someone was there. June opened her eyes, expecting to see Sam, as it was something her granddaughter would have done, but instead saw a haze of light and within it was Tom – not young Tom but her Tom, as he had been when she lost him. She sat up, stunned and rubbed her eyes. On opening them, he was still there.

"Tom?" she said.

"Hello, Beanie. It's me, yes."

She reached out and touched him. This felt so different than when he had come to her before. He was surrounded by light that radiated a calmness. Tom looked thoughtfully at her.

"Beanie," he said, "I know about Chris. I know what's happening and I can see how it's breaking everyone's heart."

"Oh Tom, it is. We really need you. We don't know if he's going to make it," said June, crying. She was still not convinced that this was happening... that it was real, but she was going with it; it was a comfort.

"That's why I'm here, darling."

"What do you mean?" she asked.

"He's not going to make it, Beanie."

June was shocked and horrified at what Tom had just said.

"Stop it Tom, we can't possibly know that."

"I can," Tom said.

"Tom, you're talking nonsense. How can you know? Why are you saying this?" June looked upset at what Tom was saying.

"I just know, June. Please believe me, but I can't bear having to tell you." Tom looked upset. June reached for his hand and kissed it.

"I don't understand why you're here telling me this, Tom?"

"Because we can save him June. We can save our grandson." Tom looked intensely at June, who knew she would do anything to let Chris live - anything at all.

"How do we do that Tom? I'll do anything it

takes."

"You can cross into this world instead of Chris."

June looked bemusedly at Tom. "What, you mean die? I can die instead of him?"

"Yes, I'll come back for you exactly one year to the minute after Chris wakes up," said Tom.

"Well, I really don't have to think twice about this," June replied. "Yes, yes, of course."

"We'll be together, Beanie and Chris will be alive and well."

"How do you know all this, though?" June was still puzzled.

"I told you, June, I really have no idea. When you come with me, it will all make sense, but you must trust me that I know... I really do just know."

June thought about the last week and a half and realised that nothing could be viewed as strange by her anymore.

"He'll wake tomorrow afternoon, Beanie; he'll be fine. At the time he wakes up, that is the time I will come for you, on the same day next year, my darling." Tom kissed her forehead. June started to say something, but he was gone.

She did not go back to sleep. She did not want to wake up in the morning and think this was all a dream, which of course it might be, but she went downstairs and made a cup of tea, sitting with the thoughts of what had just happened going round and round in her head. She would see if Chris does wake tomorrow afternoon and all is well. She will know then for sure that giving her own life up would save her grandson. She went into the lounge, put the television on and watched various night-time programmes until six-thirty, when she went for a shower and came down to prepare breakfast for everyone. She felt a knot of anticipation in her stomach, wondering if today would bring the joy Tom had promised.

One by one, the other three came downstairs and when everyone was there, June prepared breakfast for them. There was an air of sadness about all of them, they all spoke about

Chris.

Sam said, "Nan, can we go and see him later?"

"I'll speak to your Mum and Dad, Sam, to see if they are OK stepping out while we visit, as only two people are allowed at a time."

"Thanks, Nan. Yes, it won't be for long, I just want to spend a little bit of time with him."

"Alright, sweetheart, I'll phone your Mum and Dad in a minute."

June arranged for her and Samantha to visit Chris that morning for an hour. Meghan and David went down to the café and Sam sat next to her brother, telling him to hurry up and get better, as it was boring without him. June held his hand, all the time willing him to squeeze her hand or show some sign of response, but nothing changed.

Meghan and David came back after an hour. They both hugged their daughter, who was in such pain her sadness was palpable, her bond with her brother had never been stronger than now, when she felt she might lose him.

"You go back with Nanna, Sam," David said. "We promise we'll call later if and when he wakes up."

"OK, Dad."

When June and Sam arrived home, they told Jane and Paul that there was no change. They all got through the day together, hearing nothing from Meghan or David until after tea. As June was clearing plates away, the phone rang.

Sam ran to it and picked it up; they all stopped what they were doing and watched Sam intently. She suddenly broke out into a wide and unexpected grin.

"Hang on, Mum, I'll tell everyone." They were all eagerly awaiting what she had to say. "He's awake!" she said, "He's awake!" She began to cry tears of relief as June took the phone from her.

"Meg?"

"Mum!" Meghan was clearly crying at the other end. "Mum! He woke up! He's awake and he knew us! He recognised us! He can talk

Mum, he can move! They've run quite a few tests on him and he seems to have come through this with no long-term damage. Oh Mum, I just can't believe it, we've got our boy back!"

June was grinning and crying with relief.

"Meg, oh Meg, I'm so happy. When can we all see him?"

"They're moving him to a general ward this afternoon as long as his progress stays at the speed it is. They've looked at his brain and the swelling has gone. They're all a bit stunned actually, by the speed of his recovery, but I don't care, we're not questioning it, we're just so grateful for it!"

"So, we can all come when he's in the main ward?" June asked.

"Definitely. They said it would be better if visitors came after he's been transferred to a general ward, as you know how intense it is in Intensive Care and also, they like to keep it clear up here. I'll phone you all when he's been transferred."

June came off the phone and hugged her granddaughter.

"Oh, sweetheart," she said, "you have your brother back."

June thought about her conversation with Tom in the early hours and thought about the fact she had a year left. Even though it was an unbelievable scenario that she had saved Chris, she was accepting of this now, after recent events had shown her sometimes life is not normal and strange things did happen. She had no doubt that she had been given the opportunity to save her grandson and knew that over the coming year, she would make the most of that time with her family and it would also give her a chance to get all her affairs in order, to make things as easy as possible for the children, as they would be broken hearted at losing both parents. June knew that the sadness the family would have felt at losing young Chris would have been unbearable, especially for Meghan, David and Sam, so she knew the chance to save him was another blessing and gift from the love she had with Tom.

Later that day, they got the phone call to say Chris had been transferred and that they could all go in and see him. When they got to the hospital, Meghan and David hugged all of them. June saw how different her Meg looked now: her face and eyes were free of the haunted and worried look that June had seen before Chris woke. Sam ran to her brother, who was sitting up and although he looked tired, seemed to be the same old Chris. June watched her family happy and smiling, a total contrast to how it had been for the past two days. She was so grateful that she and Tom could do this for them.

They left and went back to Meghan's. David and Meghan were going to stay in the hotel until Chris was discharged, which could be as quickly as a matter of days if his progress continued the way it was going. He had been able to get out of bed and walk, although Meghan said he had been a bit weak. All was in working order and there was nothing to keep him in hospital. The doctors were bemused and said that he must have strong genes to recover so quickly from such a bad head trauma, but they also were happy for the family.

Chris went home two days later and was eventually able to go off to university and do all the things the family thought he may never be able to do. When June kissed him goodbye as he embarked on his new life, she felt at peace. Life had been nothing but strange for her in those few weeks after she lost Tom, but she accepted that she was lucky; they were lucky. They got their extra time and they got to save their grandson.

What more could either of them have asked for? And soon they would be together.

ONE YEAR LATER

June sat in Meghan's garden with a glass of champagne. Around her were Jane and

Marcus, Paul and his new girlfriend Alison, Sam and her friends and, as the guest of honour, Chris was here after his first year at university. He was telling everybody how much he had enjoyed it and was going back into a shared house rather than halls.

"A house full of boys," said Sam. "Eeew, I bet nothing will get washed or washed up," she laughed.

"Absolutely," said Chris. "Paper plates and plastic cutlery all the way. Unless you want to come, Nan, and look after us. I know you'd love the parties."

"Yes, I would, Chris. Put me in your suitcase when you go back." They all laughed.

June had booked a taxi, which was waiting. "Mum, do you have to go so early?" pleaded Meg.

"Yes, darling, I'm tired. I've had a wonderful time though." June walked to each of her children and gave them a big and lasting cuddle. She kissed each of them on the cheek and did the same to her grandchildren.

"Goodbye, my darlings," she said.

They all said goodbye and that they loved her. June got into the taxi, arrived home and looked at the paperwork she had put in the cabinet. It was all they would need to deal with her affairs, leaving them individual letters that told them not to be sad, that if they were reading this she would be with their Dad, which is something she was happy about because she had missed him so much. June looked at the clock, it was a year to the exact time since Chris had awoken from his coma. She sat in her armchair and closed her eyes, waiting for her beloved husband.

She heard his voice, "Hello, Beanie."

June opened her eyes to see her Tom; he had his hands out to her, she reached out and took them. She felt pure elation: joy like she had never known.

"Are you ready, sweetheart?" he asked her.

"Yes, Tom."

At the family party, everyone was having a

fantastic time, with laughter and happiness. The weather was warm and sunny, it was a glorious day. Suddenly, Jane said, "Hey everyone, let's play Mum and Dad's song. You know, the one I found on their record player. Mum said they always used to have a slow dance to it." She went to the laptop that was playing the music and after a few moments, the song came out over the speakers. It was a beautiful song that had transcended the years and remained as beautiful now as it had been then.

Etta James "At Last" was playing and nobody saw the couple in the corner, dancing rhythmically to it, totally in love and as one. The young couple kissed and then looked toward the people enjoying themselves, their family.

"Time to go, Beanie," Tom said when the song had finished.

June looked at her husband and, feeling his arm around her, she had never felt such bliss. They walked slowly away and ahead of them was a beautiful bright light. June and Tom headed towards it and slowly disappeared.

Their job had been done; their lives had been lived. They had created life; they had left that life to carry on for them; to live and laugh and enjoy all the things that they had themselves enjoyed and to know that their family would know that both their parents left them loved and that those parents were together: soulmates in the afterlife as they were on earth.

THE END

www.blossomspringpublishing.com